WINTER CAMPING CAPER

A COZY MYSTERY OF MURDER, SECRETS, AND SURVIVAL IN THE SNOW

COZY CORNER MYSTERIES
BOOK 3

KATHLEEN GUIRE

CHAPTER 1
A GATHERING UNDER THE STARS

THE STARS TWINKLED BRIGHTLY in the navy blue sky. I leaned back in my camping chair, inhaled and watched my breath exhale in a vapor.

"Harper, your marshmallow is on fire," Dexter said, waking me from my star-induced trance.

I shot up out of my seat and jerked my flaming marshmallow stick out of the fire.

"What ya need to do is blow on that," a voice said from the shadowy hemlocks that bordered the campsite.

I followed the directions and blew the fire out and I was rewarded with a crusty charcoal of a marshmallow, which I then waved around like a sword.

"Stop waving it around Boss, you're gonna kill someone," Zoe yelled from the chair next to mine.

"She doesn't camp much, does she?" the voice from the trees asked as he stepped out of the shadows. "Elmer's the name. Mind if I make a s'more?"

Before waiting for an answer, Elmer slung a

camping chair strap off his shoulder. In one quick motion, he pulled and unfolded the faded chair before gingerly lowering himself into it.

"Hi, Elmer," my friend and barista said as she bounced out of the chair and stuck a hand out to shake.

Elmer took it and shook it vigorously. "Nice to meet you, young lady. Nice to see the young folk camping."

I was too busy wrangling my charred marshmallow onto melty chocolate and squeezing it between two graham crackers. All the while, my labradoodle Rory pawed at my chair. Rory didn't normally beg for food, mostly because everyone at my bookstore/cafe, Cozy Corner Bookstore, had access to his doggie treats. This was different. Rory had never been camping before. Not until three weeks ago, when I had taken my first winter camping date with the handsome Detective Dexter. I hadn't actually camped all night. Because I was agoraphobic, I had only been able to stay out of my building for two or three hours at a time, depending on the day and situation. I'd stretched the time I could spend away from the Cozy Corner, which also housed my apartment, thanks to Edgar, a behavioral scientist who acted as my therapist.

"Pass the marshmallows," Aunt Mary said from across the campfire.

Zoe stood up, walked around the campfire and grabbed the basket as I crunched on my overdone s'more, which tasted divine.

"Here you go, Aunt Mary," Zoe said, while snapping a photo of me in what I'm sure was the equivalent of a gargoyle eating a s'more, glowing in the firelight, with shadows in all the wrong places.

Zoe was the social media director for the Cozy Corner and my author career. I wrote cozy mysteries and had only this semester started teaching a weekly class at Evergreen University. Zoe also managed my aunt's social media accounts for her design business and show on Home. Health. Family. Network, Sell It Or Stay.

"Elmer, we know who you are," Aunt Mary stated as she speared a marshmallow with the metal stick. She stood and moved closer to the fire and shoved the two pronged stick close to the coals before she added, "You introduce yourself every time you join us." She smiled at him, her face bathed in a warm glow as the flames flickered and played across her features.

Elmer leaned over and whispered conspiratorially to me, "Now, that is one good looking woman."

I choked on my crusty marshmallow, grabbed a water bottle Zoe handed me and took a quick swig.

"I hadn't introduced myself to this lovely lady, Mary," he said, jerking his head toward Zoe, who passed him the marshmallow basket. He took it, reached in and pulled out a plump marshmallow before continuing, "Did I ever tell you about the time a bear chased me right here in Christmas Tree Forest?"

Elmer was a regular at the campground, a retired forestry professor who'd spend the better part of his life in the woods, so it made sense that he was a regular camper year round. The forest was home to him. He parked his beat up air stream here since he'd retired. His silver hair hid under a dark beany with the Evergreen University Forestry department logo on it. He smelled of pine mixed with a spicy mix of other plants and trees I didn't recognize. Instead of a coat, he wore layers of flannel, topped with a wool sweater, and completed with a down puffy vest and khakis that had seen better days. He wore insulated leather hiking boots.

Elmer was never at a loss for words and had books of stories to share from his seventy-five plus years. He was also one of The Classics, a regular group of retired men who met daily at my cafe. Him not recognizing Zoe confirmed my aunt's suspicions he was struggling with his memory and possible dementia.

Elmer continued his bear tale while I leaned on Derek's shoulder and sipped a hot chocolate Zoe had magically produced to wash down the s'mores.

"I had a string of fish I'd caught and the bear must have gotten a whiff of them. She tore after me as I beelined it back to the campground. I wasn't going to let her take my dinner, you see..."

"Am I missing story time?" a voice outside the campfire circle asked.

"Cara, come join us," I said to the darkness.

Cara stepped into the light wearing pink hiking pants, boots, and a matching puffer jacket. She had a fancy camping chair slung over her shoulder. Cara was Aunt Mary's latest client and her home remodel was being filmed for Sell It Or Stay. Instead of staying at her home, Cara had opted for glamping some nights at Christmas Tree Forest.

This meant an elaborate set-up that looked like a living room in one tent, a bedroom in another. There was no kitchen because Cara had her meals delivered. Although Cara, like my friend Gabrielle, had money, she was down to earth and friendly. Her friendliness included lots of information about other people. Who am I kidding? Call it what it was. Gossip. Cara loved gossip.

Cara's hair cascaded down her back in waves of auburn, glowing copper in the firelight. She unfolded her chair and sat down like a fairy princess, slinging her frothy feathery scarf over her shoulder.

"Have we met, young lady? I was just telling these people…" Elmer paused as he scanned our faces with a confused look. He regained his composure, stuck out his arm and added, "As I was saying…"

Aunt Mary gave me the "I-told-you-so" look.

Dexter must have seen Elmer's distress. "You were telling us about the bear chasing you to steal your fish."

One of the many reasons I liked Dexter so much. He cared about people. And more importantly, he cared about me.

Elmer chuckled. "Oh yes, the bear."

As Elmer launched back into his tale, the trees rustled, and another figure emerged from the shadows —Anora, the state representative for the Department of Natural Resources or DNR. Her long, glossy hair flowed behind her in the light of the fire, and her sun-kissed skin glowed softly, reflecting the warmth around us.

"Sorry to interrupt your storytelling," Anora said with a smile, her bright eyes sparkling with curiosity. "I smelled the campfire from the trail and couldn't resist joining in."

"Anora! Come sit!" I waved her over, excited to have another friend around the fire.

"Glad to see you, Anora," Cara said, her tone friendly. "You're just in time for some bear stories."

Elmer perked up, adjusting his chair to face her. "You'll love this one! I was just recounting the time a bear chased me right here…"

As Anora settled into her chair, the camaraderie among us grew warmer, and I felt the weight of my agoraphobia lift, if only for this moment.

"Elmer, do you mind if I interrupt your story for a moment?" Cara asked while rising to her feet.

Elmer nodded. "Sure, honey."

"I came to tell you that there's some sort of land developer here. I think her name is Lila."

"Yes, it's Lila," a hemlock from outside of the campsite stated.

"Danny, come join us," Dexter said to the tree. As he spoke, he shined a flashlight in the direction of the talking tree. A worn ENO hammock came into view, strung tautly between two sturdy oak trees. Like a milkweed exploding, the hammock opened and spit out a long lean frame of a man cub.

As his feet hit the ground, he stumbled before righting himself.

"How long have you been hiding there?" Aunt Mary said, her eyes crinkling with amusement.

Danny straightened his man bun and then reached down to pull his worn cranberry and coconut checked flannel down. "Hiding? I wasn't hiding. The woods belong to everyone, man."

"He ate dinner with me," Dexter filled us in. "He said he needed a nap, so he strung up his hammock. He's been sleeping there for two hours."

As Danny stepped into the glow of the campfire, I smelled a distinct smell of cedar. Cara was still standing and as I glanced at her face, I could see that Danny's appearance had rendered her speechless.

Rory broke the silence by bounding from his place beside me and running round the circle, only to stop at Danny's feet. Danny reached down and patted him as Rory gave him the once over sniff.

"Sorry to interrupt but that Lila lady is something else."

"No problem," Cara stuttered. Were her cheeks red? Was it the fire? Or the handsome, rugged man with the man bun? "Continue," she added.

"Yeah, so this lady, Lila Weston, wants to commercialize Christmas Tree Forest." Instead of taking a chair Dexter offered, Danny simply squatted down, which gave Rory the advantage. Rory wasn't one to miss an opportunity to check someone's face for leftovers. So while Denny talked, Rory licked his cheeks.

"Rory, come here," I commanded.

Dexter rose and grabbed a log for the fire and Rory wandered over to investigate his activity. Thank you, Dexter.

"Commercialize?" Aunt Mary asked.

"We have the Christmas Fair here, starting the day after Thanksgiving," Zoe added.

"Yes, we have hot chocolate booths, wreath decorating…" I gazed out into the forest where less than six weeks ago, I'd been kidnapped and poisoned. I shivered. I shook off the memory and turned back to the conversation.

"Nothing like your Christmas Fair," Danny interjected.

"What does she want to do?" Elmer asked.

Danny stood and waved an arm over the forest. "Condos overlooking the forest and the lake."

"That would mean clear cutting hemlocks. Do you know how many years it takes to grow a forest?" Elmer huffed. "The incompetence and ignorance of some people."

"My house and property border the forest. What would that mean for me?" Cara asked, regaining her voice.

"I'm not sure," Aunt Mary said. "I'll look into it. But for now, I've got to get Harper home," she added as if I were a ten-year-old, instead of a bookstore owner, author and teacher.

"Yes, if we don't get Harper home, she might turn into a pumpkin," Zoe quipped with her trademark grin, her phone already angled for the perfect shot. "And this masterpiece of you mid-squat is going in the highlight reel," she added, her laughter bubbling over as she winked at me.

"I'm right here," I complained as I pulled my L.L.Bean yellow coat tighter.

"So you're like Cinderella?" Danny asked.

Clearly Danny wasn't from Evergreen Heights. Everyone here knew about "my little problem" as my father called it.

Linking arms with Dexter, we tromped down the snowy path together, his steady pace guiding me forward. Behind us, the rest of the group chatted animatedly about Lila and what her news might mean for Christmas Tree Forest. Through the trees, I heard snatches of the conversation.

"She's not messing with my view…" Cara said emphatically.

"Lila isn't going to get away with this." Danny added.

"Those trees. Do young people not know how long…" Elmer's voice trailed off into the distance.

"Thanks for walking us to the car," I said.

Dexter unlinked his arm and grabbed my free hand. The other held Rory's leash which I'd snapped on after the face licking incident. Apparently, my agoraphobia had affected Rory too. Like me, he lacked in the social skills department. Dexter and I walked the rest of the way with our hands linked, his warm grip steadying me against the cold. The soft scrape of his calloused fingers sent a quiet, grounding comfort for me, making the world feel a little less overwhelming.

Once in the parking lot, Dexter gave me a peck on the cheek and turned back to the trail to his campsite. Aunt Mary opened the SUV door for me as if I were a child while Zoe loaded the s'more and hot chocolate supplies in the back.

"Well that was a fun date," Zoe said cheerfully.

Date? A date with my barista/friend, my aunt, and half the campground. *Something had to change.* I glanced over my shoulder and watched Dexter's shadowy broad shoulders disappear into the darkness, wishing I could go with him and cuddle in front of the fire sans everyone else.

CHAPTER 2
EXPERTS AND AWKWARD INTRODUCTIONS

STORY HOUR at the Cozy Corner was a hoot this morning. Clare and Ashley, volunteer moms from Evergreen Heights, had taken over both morning story hours over a year ago when my aunt was accused of murder. I'd taken time off to investigate and prove her innocence. It was the first real murder mystery I'd solved even though I'd been writing them for years.

This morning, Clare picked *The Snowy Day* by Ezra Jack Keats. Theo and Dominic asked if they could make real snowballs outside, but settled for the styrofoam ones provided, staging an epic battle with the other kiddos. Dr. Dennis had become a regular since he'd volunteered to play Santa Claus for our Christmas series, starting with *Santa Calls*. He helped Dominic and Theo setup pillow forts while Audrey and Peregrine toddled through knocking them down.

After story hour, the kids ate powdery donut holes to represent snowballs, provided by Bea's Bakery across the street. Zoe had sent her barista-in-training to fetch them with the morning order earlier. Clare, Ashley and I had decided to take one story hour off the docket during the holidays, leaving us with one to prepare for instead of two. Although I wasn't in charge of story hour any more, I liked to attend as much as possible, not only to help, but because the Moms and kiddos had become friends.

"What do you think a ghostbuster would do with this?" Theo asked. He had positioned himself in front of my chair, holding up a round donut in front of my face.

Before answering, I took a sip of my Double Espresso. "He'd lob it at a ghost?"

"No, silly, he'd eat it for energy," he replied before stuffing the entire donut in his mouth.

"How many of those have you had?" Clare and Ashley said in unison.

Instead of answering, Theo grabbed another donut off the counter and ran out of the cafe into the bookstore, weaving through bookshelves.

"Wait for me!" Dominic yelled as he followed carrying a donut hole in each hand.

"We're cutting you two off," Clare stated with her hands on her hips. Then she turned to me and said, "Sorry."

"I'll get them before they powder up the books," Dr. Dennis offered before stuffing a donut in his mouth and heading into the bookstore.

"Thank you," I said. "It's fine. They're having fun." I shifted in my seat and glanced at my phone. No text from Dexter yet. I had a class to teach this morning, and we were heading out to Christmas Tree Forest for an inspiration hike. The assignment? Write a murder scene and the blackest moment—the point where everything seems lost, the stakes are highest, and when it feels as if nothing will work out. I'd hoped Dexter could join us and give the kids a couple of pointers on crime scenes.

"We don't want the Cozy Corner to look like a meth lab," Zoe yelled from behind the cafe counter to no one in particular. But that was Zoe, adding in her two cents on everything.

Dr. Dennis exited the book shelves with Dominic and Theo in tow, telling them a ghost busting story and wearing distinct powdery white handprints on his brown tweed suit.

"Let me clean your jacket," Clare said as she rushed toward him armed with a wet wipe.

As Dr. Dennis slid his tweed blazer off, smelling of Old Spice and pipe tobacco, Clare grabbed it and laid it on a table. She was vigorously scrubbing off the white powder when the front door opened. Jenny Murder walked in, carrying a heavy backpack.

"I'm ready, Harper." She set down her backpack and waved at Peregrine and Audrey, who toddled around the table next to me, finger painting the chairs with white powder.

Jenny scanned the room and sat down heavily next to me, her leather jacket squeaking in protest. "Have you got something going on I should investigate?"

"No," Zoe yelled above the hiss of the frother. "I told you Harper. We look like a meth lab."

"Kids in a meth lab? Should I get out my podcast equipment?" She glanced at Clare who was still scrubbing what had now turned to white goo off Dr. Dennis's jacket. "*And* The Classics? This is going to be some

Crimecaster episode. Cozy Corner Meth Lab uncovered, run by toddlers and a retired doctor of psychiatry."

Jenny laughed at her own joke while Zoe muttered under her breath at the cafe counter. "I'm not promoting that episode on social media," followed by, "Peppermint Latte is up, Jenny."

"I didn't order yet," Jenny said, standing and retrieving her drink.

"I'm that good," Zoe replied with a laugh, returning to her normal bouncy self, her spiral curls dancing in agreement.

Clare and Ashley finished rounding up their kids, supplies, purses, and headed toward the door. Clare had Dr. Dennis's jacket slung over her trendy trench coat arm. "I'm going to finish cleaning this for you and bring it back tomorrow."

Dr. Dennis chuckled. "It's no problem, Clare. I've been enjoying story hour more than you could ever know."

Dominic and Theo raced out the door while Ashley held it open and both recited "Crunch, crunch, crunch, his feet sank into the snow."

"And Zoe, if I ever ask for powdered donut holes for a snack again…" she paused as she leaned over to pick up Audrey.

Theo raced back inside skidding on the hardwood floor, "Slime her. That's what you do, Zoe." He held out an arm to demonstrate.

"Let me help you get the kids inside your van, ladies," Dr. Dennis offered. He slipped his coat off the rack and ushered Theo back out the door.

As the door closed with a blast of frigid air, I was

reminded that I needed to change into winter gear for our outdoor class.

"I need to change," I reported to Jenny and Zoe.

I glanced at my phone again. Still no text from Dexter.

"Is Sage coming?" Jenny asked.

When Jenny Murder, host of the famous Crimecaster Podcast, had moved to town a little less than a year ago, Sage, best friend and forensic photographer, and Jenny had formed a bond. When I say formed a bond, I mean Sage and Jenny argued over when to cross the line in sharing information and then made up. We'd worked on my first real murder board together. I'd had plenty of murder boards for my cozy mysteries, but that was my first actual murder. The next one was the Crimecaster Cold Case, which we'd solved right before Christmas. By solved, I mean Jenny and I had both been kidnapped by a serial killer and I'd been poisoned.

Since then, the town had licked their wounds and celebrated Christmas with more lights and gusto than normal. Now as January was ticking away, things were starting to get back to normal. I had entered a season of new normal. Winter camping dates with Dexter and meeting new camper friends like Cara, Danny the ultimate outdoorsman, Fiona the earth woman, and Anora with the super-techy RV.

Jenny had returned to town after Dexter helped her enroll her brother in a wilderness program for young men, a last-ditch effort to turn his life around before the petty gang-related crimes he was caught up in landed him in prison.

"I'm so glad your brother is doing better," I said to Jenny as she followed me up the stairs to my apartment.

"He is," Jenny replied as her Peppermint Latte sloshed over the edge of the mug. She stopped to lick the sides of the mug. "Sorry," she said, glancing at the puddle of latte on the landing.

"It's fine," I laughed. "Clare and Ashley have taught me the value of carrying wipes." I pulled a small packet of wipes out of my dress pocket, plucked one out, and leaned over to wipe the spill.

"Who are you? Adrian Monk?"

My fuzzy curls created a curtain over my eyes, blocking my view. Rory saw my distress and licked up the latte before I could clean it up.

"That's enough, Rory." I pushed him out of the way and swiped the wipe over the residue left.

Zoe and I laughed.

"I am not a defective detective," I added.

The pungent smell of Peppermint filled the hallway as I opened the door and Rory bounded inside.

———

An hour later, we were on the Hemlock Trail and students from my class were trickling in. Cassy, Robin, and Jake were the first to arrive.

"Can't wait to write my blackest moment," Robin announced, pushing a strand of black hair out of her heavily outlined eye.

"Me either," Cassy replied, bouncing on her toes, and flipping her blonde hair behind her shoulder.

"I brought my laptop," Rob added, holding up his pack as proof.

"What do you need a laptop for in the woods?" Cassy retorted.

"Hi Fiona. Class, this is Fiona. She volunteered to help us with anything we need to know about the forest."

As Fiona stepped out of a hedge of hemlocks, the strong smell of patchouli, an earthy, woody, musky scent, followed her like the cloud followed Pig Pen from Charlie Brown.

Fiona took a stand in the middle of the trail and raised her arms. "Take a deep breath kids. Breathe it in before it's gone."

"What do you mean, *gone*?" Jenny asked, as a gaggle of students joined us.

"I'll tell you what she means," Danny said from the forest.

"Who is that?" Cassy said, clinging to my L.L.Bean jacket, which squeaked along with her voice.

"Danny, please come out," I pleaded. "You're scaring my students. Some of them aren't avid outdoorsmen like you."

Before Danny appeared, we heard the clinking of metal, and what sounded like a windbreaker being folded. He stepped out of a grove of oak trees on the opposite side of the trail that Fiona had just exited. He was stuffing the windbreaker fabric into a carrier case with the emblem ENO on it.

"What Fiona means is that corporate-cat Lila is going to commercialize Christmas Tree Forest and wipe all this beauty out," he stated emphatically as he waved the bag around, his man bun nodding in agreement.

"What?" Jenny said as the class, especially the females, watched Danny with wide-eyed wonder.

"Yes, enjoy it while you can, kids." He slung the bag over his shoulder. "Oh." He turned to me. "Dex thought I could help with your little lecture."

"What do you know about murder?" I asked, crossing my arms.

"Nothing. I'm just here to help you learn about Mother Nature." Danny did a quick sideways glance to Fiona, who he probably hoped would back him up.

I was getting the feeling that Danny's knowledge of Mother Nature only extended as far as napping in a hammock and begging meals from fellow campers.

Fiona ignored him, pulled her two long silver-peppered chestnut braids over her shoulders where they landed on her burgundy prAna coat, which must have cost a pretty penny.

"I'm not here to teach you about murder," she declared. She twirled around with both arms extended. "I'm here to teach you about the Earth and its bounty."

"Thank you, Fiona and Danny." I didn't really want to thank Danny. Who was Dex, as Danny called him, to send the hammock-napping Danny to replace him?

As I pulled my phone out of my jacket pocket to look at my lesson notes, I added, "We're waiting for one more person. Sage Foster."

I scanned the students, mentally counting them to make sure I hadn't missed anyone. Cassy was staring at Danny with googly eyes, her cheeks flushed, maybe from the cold. But probably not. She needed a shove into a snowbank to cool her off.

"You mean Sage the forensic photographer?" a student asked.

"Yes," I replied.

"Triple win," Robin said. "We have a mystery writer, a crime podcaster, and a forensic photographer."

Danny cleared his throat and crossed his arms looking offended.

"And our outdoor experts, retired professor of forestry, Fiona," I quickly added, smiling and nodding to the real outdoor expert. Danny hadn't noticed my nod. He was smiling at Cassy.

CHAPTER 3
REWRITING HISTORY AND FOREST FEUDS

THE STUDENTS SPREAD out over the trail, some on the portable fishing seats Jake had brought in the back of his rumpled ancient Subaru Forester. Some paced and took notes as they crunched through the snow. Fiona flitted from student to student, offering suggestions and answering questions. She seemed to glide over the snow instead of sinking in. Her face glowed with excitement as she answered questions about which plants were poisonous and what type of tree would be a great hanging tree.

Sage took over at the word "hanging tree," describing what hanging did to the body.

Sage took a breath and began. "When someone is hanged, the sudden drop can break the neck, but often it doesn't, leaving the person to slowly suffocate as the rope tightens around the throat. The lack of oxygen causes the skin to turn a bluish color, and blood vessels can burst in the eyes. It's a cruel, agonizing way to die, and the body is left twisted and limp as gravity does its work."

Robin raised a hand. "So, is that why some hangings are done with a longer drop—to make it quicker?"

Sage nodded, "Exactly. The longer drop is meant to ensure a swift neck break, which is supposed to be more humane, though it doesn't always go as planned."

After Sage's short lecture, Jenny took over. She shared three episodes of her Crimecaster Podcast she thought would help the students not only write the murder, but the blackest moment for the amateur sleuth in their story.

"If you want to explore how your teacher handled the blackest moment, listen to season nine, episode twelve, and season ten episode eleven." She laughed.

"The murderer shot Jenny right here." I motioned to the spot where Jenny had stood when Eustace had shot her, trying to get the attention off myself and on to her.

"Didn't the murderer shoot himself in season nine and episode twelve?" Robin asked.

"Yes, didn't the bullet ricochet off a rock?" Cassy added, checking out the snow-covered boulders on the edges of the trail with wide eyes.

Jake pushed his glasses up and said, "When a bullet hits a hard surface like a rock, it can ricochet, or bounce off, depending on the angle. If the impact angle is just right, the bullet can rebound back toward the shooter with much of its speed intact. It's all about how momentum and angles work together."

"Yes, it was the rock right behind Robin," I said.

The group turned and examined the rock.

"The murderer stood right here," I said, stepping to the exact spot where Eustace had aimed and shot Jenny.

"And he shot *you!*" Jenny said, as she pulled her phone out of her pocket.

"I recorded it all."

Ethan stood a little apart from the group, adjusting his thick navy parka and pulling his knit beanie down over his ears to shield against the cold. His breath formed small puffs in the air as he spoke, his wide eyes betraying his curiosity mixed with skepticism. A new student and an aspiring author, Ethan hadn't quite warmed up to the class yet, but the prospect of listening to real-life crime stories clearly piqued his interest. "My teacher was shot at. Awesome," he said, a trace of awe creeping into his voice.

Ryan, bundled up in a dark green puffer jacket with a plaid scarf wrapped around his neck, leaned forward with interest. His cheeks were flushed from the cold, and a few strands of dark hair escaped from beneath his gray beanie. Known for being the kind of student who remembered every interesting fact, Ryan's eyes lit up at the mention of previous episodes.

"And poisoned," Jenny added.

He quickly chimed in, "What were those episodes again?" He was clearly hooked, eager for all the gritty details.

"Guys, always a step behind. I bet neither of you have ever listened to a podcast," Cassy said, while adjusting her pink hat over her ears.

"Neanderthals," Robin added.

"Let's not resort to name calling, children," Fiona said. "Mother Earth is all about acceptance and love."

And murder, I thought to myself. It wouldn't help to say that out loud. Instead I stated, "We can listen to the podcast episode when we gather at the Cozy Corner."

Jenny recited the seasons and episodes again, students eagerly pulling out phones to jot notes or queue up her podcast. The vibe was macabre, yet oddly joyful, like a creepy campfire story that left everyone grinning.

As promised, I snapped a few photos for Zoe and sent them off. Nearby, a few students gathered under an ancient hemlock, its massive branches casting deep, mossy shadows. They whispered excitedly, caught up in the spooky charm of the lesson.

"I bet I could help you," Danny said, inserting himself into the semicircle of students.

Jenny and I locked eyes for a second and I put a hand up to silence Robin, who was describing her murderer to me and the use of a hanging tree prescribed by Fiona. I wanted to see what Danny could bring to the table before continuing to judge him so harshly.

Where did that come from? I was displacing my anger. I didn't normally show my anger. Instead, it simmered under the surface. I was the little teapot who got all steamed up, and I poured out by helping other people and ignoring my own feelings.

"This is a shagbark hickory," Danny said, patting the bark of the tree. Danny crossed his arms, his breath puffing out in the cold. "Man, if those corporate suits don't chill, these trees are gonna be history, and we'll be here gasping for air while the ozone's toast." He grabbed his throat for effect and held his breath.

The group of students stared at him in wonder and horror.

"Don't be ridiculous," Fiona said as she stomped through the snow to the tree. "This is a hemlock. She pointed to the trail sign. We are on the Hemlock Trail. Forest covers seventy-nine percent of this state. We have plenty of fresh air to breathe." Fiona paused and took a deep breath, extending her arms into Tree Pose.

She balanced on one leg, the sole of her other foot pressed against her inner thigh, her arms reaching upward toward the sky as if drawing strength from the earth below. It was a fitting pose for a nature-loving soul, grounding herself like the very trees she cared about.

The students breathed an audible sigh of relief.

Danny turned as red as a male cardinal before rushing up the snowbank into the forest, with his hammock sack slung over his back.

I scanned the class to get a read on them before saying, "Let's not judge Danny too harshly. We all make mistakes. We're here to learn, right?" By the looks on the female students' faces, they wanted to learn more about handsome man-bunned Danny, whether he knew the species of trees or not.

"We will be wrapping up here in fifteen minutes and relocating to the Cozy Corner to grab hot chocolate or coffee and discuss your ideas. Jenny will be on hand, as well as Sage and I, to help you."

I'd asked Zoe to pull out some of yesterday's baked goods and make a batch of hot chocolate and coffee for the class, on the house. I knew these students had invested what little money they had left over after tuition on food and housing. I wanted this class to be a blessing, not another burden. I'd seen the embarrassed looks when a few of the students attended a book club and didn't have the funds for fancy coffee drinks. I didn't want them to feel as if meeting at the Cozy Corner was a money-making scheme for me, when it was actually for my comfort so I could lessen my time out and extend the class discussion.

As we were loading up in our vehicles, Elmer rushed out of the woods into the parking lot.

"I found the photos of the bird!" he shouted in Fiona's direction. His boots slid in the slush to a stop barely missing his forehead making contact with a side-view mirror on an SUV.

"Well look at all you lovely young people." He stuck a hand out to steady himself, hanging on the mirror and bending it out of alignment.

"I'm Elmer…" he said to me.

Fiona interrupted him with, "Let's not talk about the bird here. These kids need to get back to class."

"Which bird?" I asked Elmer. Knowing what my aunt had told me about her suspicions concerning dementia and how people sometimes treated others with mental illnesses, I didn't want him to feel we didn't care.

"Oh it's a…" He lifted a hat and scratched his head. "I have lots of research. Oh, and a photo or two."

"We can talk about this later," Fiona interjected.

———

By the time we'd settled at the Cozy Corner, Zoe had hot chocolate and goodies ready.

Ethan raised a fist as he grabbed a donut with one hand. "Best class ever. Murder and food!"

Jenny sat at a center table and pulled a speaker out of her bag and cued up the podcast. The Classics lingered, nursing coffees and whispering to each other. When Jenny pushed play, The Classics quieted, followed by a loud squeaking as they moved their chairs closer to the speaker.

The podcast began with the Crimecaster Theme Music playing. As it faded out, we heard Jenny Murder's voice come across the speakers:[Crimecaster Theme Music Plays, then fades out]

Jenny Murder: "Welcome back, Crimecasters. I'm your host, Jenny Murder, and today's story nearly cost me more than just a headline. This is an episode I didn't plan on recording—or living through. Let me take you back to where it all went down..."

[Sound of crunching leaves and forest ambiance fades in]

Jenny Murder: "We were deep on the trail, pressing Gabrielle for answers when I heard it—a whoosh to my left. And then, pain. I crumpled to the ground, just as the bark of a hemlock splintered near me. 'Hit the dirt!' Harper shouted."

[Sound effect of rapid movement, followed by a shot ringing out]

Jenny Murder: "Gabrielle and I hit the dirt and crawled back to a boulder, hearts racing, adrenaline spiking. But we weren't alone."

[Sound of Eustace's voice, sneering]
Eustace: "I knew you'd figure it out eventually, Miss Murder. You and your little mystery mind."
Jenny Murder: "Another shot rang out. It was then my brain caught up with the fact that someone was shooting at us. I felt the warmth of blood on my arm. A graze, but it hurt like—well, let's just say it hurt. Harper, always quick on her feet, tied a bandana around my arm to stop the bleeding."
[Sound of another shot ricocheting off the boulder]
Jenny Murder: "Eustace kept talking, like a cornered animal who still thought he could bite."
Eustace: "I thought I paid you off, Miss Murder. The deal was you'd stop investigating."
Jenny Murder: "But then…"
[Eustace screams]
Jenny Murder: "The idiot shot himself. Talk about poetic justice."
[Sound of shuffling]
Jenny Murder: "And just like that, Gabrielle was gone —vanished from my side. I peered around the boulder and saw her tending to Eustace, pressing on his shoulder wound. Her voice trembled as she demanded answers."
[Sound of Gabrielle's voice, shaky]
Gabrielle: "Is it true? You killed Horace and blamed me so you could inherit the estate?"
Jenny Murder: "I could hear the pain in her voice. Eustace's reply came, dripping with condescension."
Eustace: "It should have been mine in the first place. Not some girl from the gutter. The Vanderhilts used to have standards."

[Sound of a gun being cocked]

Jenny Murder: "Gabrielle's arms shook as she aimed the gun at Eustace. Her voice cracked as she spoke."

Gabrielle: "I don't care about the estate. I just wanted someone to care about me. Do you know what it's like to live with a man who beats you every day, who tells you that you're worthless?"

Jenny Murder: "Harper was edging closer, desperate to diffuse the situation."

Harper: "Gabrielle, you didn't commit any crime. The estate is yours. If you shoot him, you'll lose it all."

Jenny Murder: "But Gabrielle swung the gun toward Harper. She was on the edge, and Harper tried to reason with her."

Gabrielle: "You weren't faking, were you, Harper? You really cared."

Jenny Murder: "But Eustace, the slippery snake, lunged. He kicked Gabrielle's knees out from under her, and the gun went off."

[Sound of a gunshot]

Jenny Murder: "The next thing I knew, I was on the ground, clutching my shoulder, and Eustace was scrambling over Gabrielle like the true coward he was."

[Sound of struggling and heavy breathing]

At this point, Elmer rushed in. "Sorry I'm late. I got into an argument with that earth woman." He stopped and wiped his feet and petted Rory, who met him at the door. Jenny paused the podcast so everyone could greet him.

"Hello Elmer," Edgar said in a soothing tone. He stood and pulled a chair and motioned for him to sit down.

"Are you listening to the Crimecaster Podcast?" Elmer asked. "I love that show. I think I met the host once. Or maybe she interviewed me."

He scanned the room and his gaze landed on Jenny. "There she is. Miss Murder."

"Hello, Elmer," Jenny replied.

"Hey, Boss," Zoe yelled from behind the cafe counter. "Since everyone in the building is listening to the podcast, why don't we play it on the sound system?"

"That's a great idea, Zoe." I turned to address Jenny. "Can you help her make that happen?"

Jake stood. "I can handle it."

"Thanks, Jake," Jenny replied. She handed her phone to him.

"How about some fresh coffees for The Classics?" I added. "On the house."

Jake pushed a few apps on the phone and the podcast restarted on the sound system, replacing the soft jazz that had been plunking away in the background.

The cafe was silent except for the rustling of coats being removed and the clinking of mugs, while the rich voice of Jenny Murder crackled over the sound system, capturing everyone's attention. The air was thick with the earthy aroma of freshly brewed coffee and a hint of cinnamon, mingling with the sweet scent of pastries.

Warmth radiated from the steaming mugs. A cozy glow settled over the crowded tables as listeners leaned in, hanging on every word like it was an old-time radio show.

Jenny Murder: "And just when I thought it was over, there it was—Elmer's gasping confession."
Gabrielle: "You killed your brother and the housekeeper, didn't you?"
Eustace: "I should have gotten the estate."
Jenny Murder: "And that's when it clicked. The renovation on Gabrielle's house—it wasn't just construction."
[Sound of Jenny yelling]
Jenny Murder: "The hot tub, Harper! It was supposed to be installed by the old conservatory, wasn't it?"
Harper: "Yes! That's where he buried the bodies!"
Eustace: "Shut up! I'm going to kill you all!"
Jenny Murder: "But before he could make good on his threat, a voice rang out."
[Sound of Dexter's calm but firm voice]
Dexter: "I don't think so. Drop the gun, Eustace."
Jenny Murder: "And then, like angels of justice, the police swarmed out from behind the hemlocks."
[Eustace curses, scuffling sounds, then silence]
Jenny Murder: "Eustace was finally in custody, and the truth had come to light. But remember, Crimecasters, sometimes justice comes at a high price. We all walked away that day, but with more scars than we started."
[Crimecaster theme music fades back in]

**Jenny Murder: "Tune in next time, and don't forget—
you never know when you'll stumble upon a clue... or
a killer."
[Sound fades out]**

I chuckled under my breath. Leave it to Jenny to change the story making herself the heroine who was shot twice. I'd never listened to that episode because I'd lived it.

Ryan raised his hand. "I thought you got shot, Harper."

Jenny blushed, realizing her blunder. She likes to be the center of attention and report what she learned as fact before corroboration. Apparently, she also likes to rewrite history to make herself look good.

"Yes, it sounds as if you took some creative license with the podcast," Edgar said. "If you want the rest of the story, ask your teacher."

Jenny put her phone in her backpack and slung it over her shoulder. "Thanks for listening. Don't forget to subscribe so you don't miss an episode."

She walked toward the front door with her head down, like Rory did when he was ashamed of stealing food from the table. She stopped to pat Rory on the head and pushed the door open, letting in a frigid blast of air.

Detective Dexter entered while she exited and she mumbled a "hello" before walking down the sidewalk.

"Sorry I missed the lecture," he said to no one and

everyone. "I had to arrange some things for a town council meeting this evening."

"It's about the bird, isn't it?" Elmer asked while standing to his feet and patting his flannel shirt. "I'd better go home and get my notes."

"No Elmer," Dexter took three long strides to him and patted him on the shoulder. "It's not a class lecture. It's a meeting with Coldwater Corp and Lila Weston."

"The people who want to commercialize Christmas Tree Forest?" Zoe yelled from behind the cafe counter.

CHAPTER 4
POPCORN, PROTESTS, AND PROPOSALS

THE CLASS ENDED with students asking me questions about my involvement with the murder on the set of my aunt's show Sell It Or Stay and the College Co-ed murders.

As most of the students packed up to leave, I overheard Cassy tell Ethan, "She has a murder board in her apartment."

"That's so cool," he replied, eyeing me with new respect.

"That board is for outlining my novels," I interjected. "And speaking of novels, make sure you turn in your draft next Monday for your murder scene and the blackest moment."

Instead of leaving like the rest of the class, Jake, Robin, Cassy, and the two newest of their group, Ethan and Ryan, opted to stay. It was just past twelve-thirty and the familiar buzz of conversation filled the air as the five students gathered to work on their assignment, fueled by caffeine and creativity.

They commandeered one of the large tables near the window, their laughter ringing out above the soft chatter. I sipped my coffee, leaning back in my chair, admiring the community the Cozy Corner created.

Dr. Dennis and Edgar ambled over to the students' table.

"Have any wisdom for us, Edgar or Dr. Dennis?" Robin asked, her hand poised with pen ready. "I need all the help I can get."

"Speak for yourself," Cassy added with a wink. "I am more focused on solving murders than absorbing wisdom!"

"Ah, a young detective in our midst!" Dr. Dennis announced, adjusting his glasses and taking a seat at the table. "Just be careful not to get too carried away. Fictional murders can be much easier to navigate than real-life dilemmas."

"What's this about a murder club?" asked Larry, one of the other Classics, his weathered face lighting up with curiosity as he joined them. He leaned in, eager to hear more. "Are you kids planning to hunt down real criminals?"

"We're just brainstorming, Mr. Larry," Cassy explained, excitement bubbling in her voice. "Robin had the brilliant idea of starting a club where we can learn about cold cases and maybe even solve a few mysteries!"

"I think it's a fantastic idea!" Larry replied, nodding sagely. "As long as you keep it light-hearted. Remember, there's a fine line between curiosity and becoming too involved in someone else's tragedy."

"Right, like Jenny's Crimecaster Podcast," Robin

added. "Some of them go a bit overboard with the details."

I'm sure she was referring to Jenny's episodes on the College Co-ed Killer Case, where she shared information that ultimately connected to the murder of Willow, a college student and barista-in-training.

Edgar chuckled, leaning back in his chair and stretching his long legs out in front of him. "It's true. But they can also be a great way to explore human behavior, as long as you don't forget the importance of compassion."

"Exactly!" Dr. Dennis interjected. "Understanding motivations and the psychological aspects of crime can be fascinating. Perhaps you'd like to incorporate some of those discussions into your club, Jake?"

"Yeah, that'd be great," Jake replied. "I'm definitely up for that. It might even make for some better plots!"

As I observed the lively exchange, I felt a surge of pride. My students were thriving in this creative environment, and it warmed my heart to see them engage with The Classics, who were more than willing to share their experiences and insights.

"Just remember, the best mysteries often come from real-life inspirations," I added, leaning over to join their conversation. "And the more you learn about the human experience, the richer your stories will become."

"Speaking of inspiration, Harper," Edgar said, "are you still planning to host that workshop on developing believable characters?"

"Absolutely! I'll announce the date soon," I promised, excitement bubbling within me at the thought of sharing. "I'd love for you all to join us. It'll be a great opportunity to dive deeper into character development."

Just then, Aunt Mary entered with a fresh tray of pastries, her eyes sparkling with mischief. "What's all this talk about murder? If you kids need any tips, I have a few stories from my design clients that might surprise you!"

The laughter erupted again, a joyful sound that filled the cafe. Surrounded by the camaraderie of students and friends, I felt a renewed sense of purpose. This was more than just a cafe. It was a hub of creativity, learning, and the ever-pulsating heart of my life as a cozy mystery writer.

During the lively discussion and plans for the murder club, Dexter had been chatting with Elmer. With Elmer and Robin on their way out the door, Dexter joined me. Five minutes later, Dexter and I made our way to the second floor and camped out on the leather couches. I sipped the water bottle Zoe handed me before promising to order a late lunch and make us some fresh coffees.

I relaxed against the back of the couch, taking in a deep breath. "I think I need a nap."

"Are you still enjoying teaching?" Dexter asked, scooting closer until our shoulders nearly touched.

"Yes, I am," I replied, my voice softening. "I've just had a lot going on lately," I added, letting him in on the reason behind my tired eyes.

He raised a brow, giving my hand a gentle squeeze. "You're writing a new novel, aren't you?"

I smiled, feeling a bit lighter. "I am, and it's been a lot of fun to write." I let out a small laugh. "But it also means I'm up at four-thirty most mornings to get it all done."

Dexter shook his head with a knowing look. "And you've had so much more outside time," he noted, a flicker of concern in his eyes. "Which I'm sure only adds to your stress load."

I nodded my head in agreement, but didn't have the energy to answer. Not to mention, the lecture today on the trail was triggering. I'd made it a point not to let Christmas Tree Forest be painted in bad memories. It had been my favorite place as a child. It had been one place I was happy with my parents, and Aunt Mary had continued the tradition by taking me there often. In the winter, the snow sat like melting icing on the hemlocks, giving it a magical feel. But, I'd confronted two killers there and had almost been killed myself. The Christmas fair had been my favorite event. My mind was on three train tracks at the same time.

I sat straight up just as Zoe called, "Boss, I've got your coffees."

Zoe didn't need to deliver my coffee. She had employees to do that. She just couldn't resist seeing what I was up to, snapping a photo, and posting it on social media, or at least talking about it loudly. I couldn't complain. Zoe had been there for me when my agoraphobia was the worst. When Aunt Mary had handed me the keys to the building housing the cafe and bookstore, plus my apartment, I hadn't left the building for the first three months. Zoe had handled everything from setting up a contract with Bea's Bakery across the street to managing equipment and booking deliveries. Sure, I had helped inside the building, but I hadn't even been able to manage going outside to direct truck deliveries to the back brick alley. Not to mention, Zoe could make The Grinch smile and anyone's heart grow two sizes.

I patted the couch cushion next to me. "Join us," I said, my words slurred.

"Boss, if I didn't know any better, I'd say you were hitting the bottle."

"You know I don't drink." I grabbed the tiny mug with the words "Deja Brew" stamped on it and took a sip. "I just need some of this."

"What have you had to eat today?" she prodded, as she handed Dexter his Red-Eye.

"Eat?" I laughed at the question. Who had time to eat? "I had a s'more last night."

"I'm going to see what happened to the food I ordered you." She sank into a leather armchair and pulled her phone out of her pocket. "It will be here in five." She stood and shoved her phone back in her apron pocket. "I'll text you when it gets here." She turned to Dexter. "You make sure she eats."

"Will do," Dexter replied.

After a few sips of the strong espresso, I revived slightly. Jake delivered Rory, fresh from his walk. Someone had taken the time to towel him dry.

"Zoe told me to let you know I was back with Rory," Jake said, glancing around the room as he spoke.

"Jake, sit a moment," I replied, gesturing to the chair beside me.

He raised an eyebrow but shrugged and took a seat. "What's up?"

"I just have one question," I began, leaning forward. "Do you know Danny?"

"Well, yes, I met him today," Jake answered, his tone cautious.

"I mean, did you know him before today?" I pressed.

"No," Jake replied, frowning slightly. "I get the feeling he's new here."

Dexter leaned closer, joining the conversation with a nod. "Yeah, I get the feeling he doesn't live here—or plan to."

Jake's eyes narrowed. "Why are you asking me?" he said, his voice edged with interest.

"Because he's about your age, right? Just wondering if he's a student," I explained, my gaze steady on him.

"No, I've never seen him on campus, if that's what you're asking," Jake responded, rubbing the back of his neck.

"Why?" Dexter asked, folding his arms as he studied me.

"Well, something about him just doesn't make sense," I admitted, my fingers drumming lightly on the coffee table.

Dexter leaned in, his gaze narrowing. "What, because he's some sort of earth lover, like Fiona?"

"That's just the thing," I replied, shaking my head. "He's not."

Jake let out a chuckle. "Yeah, he called a hemlock a shagbark hickory today in class. Anyone who lives in Evergreen Heights knows what a hemlock is—*even* computer science majors like me." He flashed a quick grin.

"He just showed up at the Christmas Tree Campground about a week ago, mooching off everyone," Dexter said.

My phone buzzed.

A text from Zoe.

Robin's here with the food.

Robin, Jake's sister, worked at The Sandwich Shop. She'd introduced me to Professor Kaitlin, who had invited me to guest lecture at Evergreen University.

I took the last sip of my Double Espresso and grabbed Dexter's mug. "Let's go downstairs, shall we?"

Robin met us at the bottom of the stairs. "Hey!"

"Hi Robin, we're going to eat down here."

"Great. I brought Jake a sandwich. He forgets to eat sometimes."

"See Boss, you're not the only one," Zoe said as she whizzed past us with a tray of coffees.

We grabbed a table near the window. The snow was falling, blanketing the sidewalks and streets in a soft, untouched layer, turning the world beyond the window into a quiet winter wonderland.

"How did you know he was still here?" I asked as I peeled The Sandwich Shop sticker off the paper bag closure, releasing the pleasant aroma of turkey and cranberry, my favorite wrap.

Robin slid a chair over from the table beside us. "It's an app. Jake put it on both our phones during the College Co-ed Killer Case. We know where the other is at all times."

"Can anyone get that app?" I asked, showing my technology ignorance.

"I have it on you, Boss!" Zoe said, joining us and placing two steaming mugs on the table.

"What?"

"Yeah, after you were kidnapped last year, Jake helped your Aunt Mary get it. So I decided to get it too."

"We didn't order any more coffee," I snapped, swallowing my frustration. I wasn't a child who needed constant supervision. I'd come so far, pushing myself to spend more time outside, even when it felt overwhelming. But no matter how much progress I made, I couldn't shake the feeling of being that little girl who got lost at the carnival.

While everyone else seemed to know exactly where they were going and what to do, I was stumbling around in sensory overload, trying to dodge the flashing lights and blaring sounds. It was as if I was stuck on the outskirts, missing out on the world unfolding around me—forgetting to check off tasks, neglecting to eat, just struggling to keep up.

"These are for Robin and Jake," Zoe stated, and then bounced away.

As I pulled the rest of the orders out of the bag and passed them around, Dexter handed out napkins.

"There's a town hall meeting tonight," Jake said, peering at his phone screen.

"Yes, that's why I missed class," Dexter said. "Apparently this Lila Weston thinks she'll need police protection."

I wiped a piece of cranberry off my chin. "So that's going to be you?"

Dexter set down his Reuben sandwich and took a sip of his water before answering. "Yes."

Robin's eyes widened as she studied Dexter's ruggedly handsome face. "Aren't you the head detective?"

"I am."

"Then why are you on babysitting duty for a Coldwater Corp executive?" Jake asked, without looking up from his phone.

Before Dexter could answer, Jake continued reading from his phone screen. "Listen to this."

Today, I crossed paths with Lila Weston—yes, *that* Lila Weston. The one with the sleek ponytail, outdoor-chic style, and the scent of pine and vanilla trailing behind her like a perfectly curated fragrance ad. She's here with big plans to "enhance" our Christmas Tree Forest... but I can't help wondering if her idea of enhancement involves stripping away the very soul of the land.

Our forest isn't some backdrop for her holiday attraction—it's a living, breathing community. And while Lila might look good in her stylish puffer vests and tailored cargo pants, I'm not convinced she's the one to protect what truly matters here.

#ProtectOurForest #NatureNotProfit #LilaWeston #ChristmasTreeForest #AmbitionVsConservation #MotherEarthMatters #SustainableLiving #LeaveNoTrace #NotForSale

Robin grabbed her phone. "Is that Fiona? The earthy lady who smells like patchouli and puts Danny man-bun in his place?"

"That was on Instagram," he said.

"She has a post on TikTok too." He held up his phone, and the video played.

The video began with Fiona standing in the snow covered forest pointing to the trees.

"Hey, everyone! So, guess who I ran into today… Lila Weston. Yep, the woman with the sleek ponytail and that 'I'm ready to conquer the world' look, dressed head-to-toe in outdoor chic. You know, fitted fleece jacket, trendy puffer vest—basically, looking like she just stepped out of an Instagram ad for 'luxury wilderness.' Oh, and she even smells like pine and vanilla, go figure." **[Fiona rolls her eyes, then turns the camera back to herself.]**

"But let's get real for a sec. Lila's here to 'transform' our Christmas Tree Forest into some kind of holiday wonderland. But when she says 'transform,' I hear 'exploit.' I mean, does she even understand what this place means to us?" **[Camera pans to a close-up of Fiona holding a pinecone.]**

"These trees aren't just decorations. This forest is alive. It's not here to be some backdrop for her idea of a 'magical' attraction. We have enough commercialized spaces—this is one of the few sacred places left. And, sorry, but no amount of trendy cargo pants or charming speeches is gonna convince me otherwise." **[Fiona**

shakes her head and the video zooms out to show the forest again.]
"We need to protect this place, not turn it into another profit-driven playground. Who's with me?"

"So maybe Lila needs protecting?" I asked.

"Not from Fiona," Dexter said. "She has no record."

"All of her other posts are educational," Robin said. "About trees and wildlife. She's pretty chill like she was this morning in class."

"Regardless, that's what I'm doing this evening," Dexter replied as he gathered his sandwich wrapper and water bottle. "You coming?"

"I have to come for my journalism course and write a piece on it," Robin answered.

"Not me," Jake said, "but I think Cassy is and a few of your other students."

"I'm not." I wished I could go, but I'd used all my outside time up already.

"I'm watching via zoom," Jake added. "I could come here if you'd like to watch with me?"

"Yes, I'd like that. Thank you, Jake."

———

Later that evening, Jake set up the meeting on the TV in my apartment. I popped popcorn because I didn't know what was socially acceptable for viewing a town hall meeting on Zoom. I used Zoom for meetings with my editor, Leslie, who was super formal, but the students who had begged to join us seemed relaxed.

Cassy opted to join us instead of attending live.

Ethan and Ryan as well. I think they just wanted a glimpse of my murder board, which had my latest novel plotted on it.

While we snacked on popcorn and munched on peanut butter cookies, the meeting started with the mayor introducing Lila Weston.

"Hello everyone, thanks for welcoming me to your wonderful little town of Evergreen Heights."

A pattering of light applause.

"What I'd like to do tonight is give you the vision I have for expanding the tourism at Christmas Tree Forest and boosting the economy of your town." A screen dropped from the ceiling and a glossy photo of Christmas Tree Forest appeared with the pristine Starlight Lake in the center.

Lila gazed at the screen for a moment to let the viewers soak it all in. In the literary world, we called this the dramatic pause.

She clicked the remote and another photo of Christmas Tree Forest appeared complete with chalets and a large condo surrounded the lake.

Upset voices grumbled in the background and someone yelled, "You can't do that!"

Then Dexter's voice said, "Let's let Mrs. Weston finish her presentation."

"Yes, I'll reserve time for a Q and A at the end." Lila answered, while flipping her ponytail.

The voice continued, "I was supposed to give a lecture on the bird."

Elmer rushed up to the stage, shuffling papers. He joined Lila at the podium. "You're a pretty lady, aren't ya, but I need to lecture my students on the Cerulean

Warblers, so if you don't mind leaving the lecture hall."

"Detective, if you could do your job?" Lila stated, the frustration clear in her voice.

Instead of Dexter hopping on the stage, Danny appeared, whispering to Elmer. The mic didn't pick up the conversation, but whatever he said, it got Elmer off the stage.

What the mic picked up was Lila whispering, "Thanks, son."

CHAPTER 5
TRIGGERS AND DETERMINATION

I JUMPED up from my seat on the sectional and my popcorn flew up in the air and landed in convenient places for Rory to gobble up. "Did Lila call him son?"

"Did she mean son, as in 'hey son' or like biological or adopted?" Cassy asked.

"Well, there's a twist," Jake added.

Ethan grabbed a peanut butter cookie and stuffed it in his mouth. After swallowing it whole, he said, "I thought the more interesting part was the nutty professor jumping on the stage."

"He's not a nutty professor." I sat back down. "That's Elmer. He is a retired forestry professor from Evergreen University."

"I think he has what my grandma does," Jake said as he lowered the volume on the meeting so we could continue to chat.

As Lila's presentation droned on like a low irritating hum in the background, my students talked about memory loss, dementia, and Alzheimer's in their family.

There were no other incidents during Lila's presentation. If anyone else from the audience complained, we couldn't hear them. She wrapped up with a smile and a timeline, promising the first wave of construction being finished in time for the Christmas Fair.

"The Meeting Has Ended" flashed across the screen, unnoticed by everyone except Jake, who leaned over to shut down the computer. The room was still buzzing with lingering conversations, though the meeting had wrapped up nearly ten minutes ago. Cassy and I moved around the room, tidying up as the chatter continued. We gathered plates, glasses, and mugs, carrying them to the kitchen island.

"I can load the dishwasher," she said as I set the last bowl down on the counter.

My phone buzzed, and I picked it up. A text from Aunt Mary.

"Thank you," I said to Cassy before I crossed the living room and ran up the stairs to my bedroom/office.

Aunt Mary:

> Did you see Elmer at the meeting? I'm
> worried about him. He's missing.

Me:

> What?

Instead of answering my text, Aunt Mary called me.

"Harper, Elmer is missing."

I fiddled with my computer mouse to give my hands something to do. "What do you mean 'missing'?"

"Hey Harper," Jake yelled from the bottom of the stairs. "I'm going to walk Rory and Cassy wants to know where the vacuum is."

I put the phone down so as not to yell in Aunt Mary's ear. "Thank you. The vacuum is in the laundry room."

What was up with Cassy? She didn't normally have a domestic bone in her pink manicured fingers. What was it she told Jake when we were doing some research in the library? "This isn't 1950. Women aren't here to grab your coffee, Jake. Get it yourself."

I picked up the phone. "Sorry Aunt Mary, I'm back."

"Yes, after Danny helped Elmer off the stage, he exited a side door and..."

"Did you try his house? Or the campground?" I asked, thinking like a detective. Then I changed my approach. "What about a favorite place?"

"I'm on my way to the Christmas Tree Forest Campground right now," she said.

"Can you get Jenny to try his house?" I asked. "I'll call Edgar and see if any of The Classics have seen him."

Aunt Mary wouldn't ask me to join her impromptu search team outside of the building, but I could help in my own way.

The town hall was two blocks from the Cozy Corner.

"I gotta go Aunt Mary, I'll let you know what I find out." I hung up without giving her a chance to respond, before I ran down the stairs.

"Ethan, Ryan, Jake! Elmer is missing. Do you think you can search the few blocks around the town hall and see if you can find him?"

Jake clipped the leash on Rory's collar, which flipped a switch in the labradoodle, who pulled him toward the door.

"I've got your coats," Ethan yelled as he grabbed Jake and Ryan's coats off the racks and opened the apartment door. Rory rushed out the door, pulling Jake along as Ethan held open the door.

"My grandma does this sometimes," Ryan said over his shoulder as he grabbed his coat from Ethan's hand and followed him out the open door. As he pulled it shut, he promised, "We'll find Elmer."

As soon as he closed the door, it opened again. I wondered if they forgot something or found Elmer in the stairwell.

Instead of the college students, Jenny rushed in. "Did you see the meeting?"

Cassy turned from the sink and asked, "Did we miss any juicy parts?"

"You saw Elmer try to take over and lecture his 'students'? Right?"

"Jenny, he's missing."

"Elmer?"

"Yes, I'm sure you passed Jake, Ethan, and Ryan in the stairwell. They're going to search for him."

Jenny set her backpack down on the island. "Oh no, what can I do to help?"

"My aunt is driving to the campground to see if she can find him there. Do you mind driving over to check his house?"

Cassy joined us at the island, wiping her hands on a dishtowel. "I'll come with you Jenny."

Aunt Mary had texted me his address, and I shared it with Jenny. Once they'd gone, I called Edgar.

"Are you okay?" he asked after saying hello.

"It's not me this time. Elmer is missing." I didn't blame him for thinking I was the one who needed help. I'd called him many times in the past, needing him to come over because I was having a panic attack or fill-in-the-blank.

"I'll call some of the other Classics and see if any of them have seen him."

"Thank you," I said.

"I'll let you know if I find him."

I clicked the end call button and looked around my empty apartment. The dishes were loaded in the dishwasher. The counters wiped. I decided because I could do nothing else to help with Elmer at the moment, to grab the vacuum and finish cleaning up.

I was running the vacuum over cookie crumbs Rory had missed when my phone vibrated in my pocket. I switched off the vacuum and leaned on the coffee table.

It was a text from Dexter:

Call me.

Followed in quick succession by one from Sage:

I have bad news.

Then one from Jenny:

We found Elmer. He's dead.

I called Dexter immediately after texting Sage and Jenny back with:

Elmer's dead?

Dexter answered on the fourth ring.

"Harper, I'm here at Elmer's house with Sage, Jenny, and Cassy. They told me you were on assignment from your aunt to look for Elmer." He paused and sucked in a breath.

"He's dead," I said, filling in the pause.

"How did you…" I couldn't see him, but I could imagine he was glaring at Jenny.

"Jenny texted me," I continued. "What happened?"

"We found him in his study after we got a tip from your aunt."

"Why did my aunt think he was missing if he just went home after the town hall meeting?"

"Your aunt must have been too upset about what happened after the meeting and failed to tell you…"

My phone buzzed, and I held it back from my ear and read the text from Jenny:

Your aunt had Elmer admitted to the
psych ward after his little stunt at the
town hall meeting.

I put the phone back up to my ear. "He escaped from the hospital?"

Instead of answering me, he said, "Jenny, I'm going to need your phone."

I'm sure Jenny huffed and made a few remarks before promising, "I won't text her any more details."

With Dexter refusing to share details about the ongoing investigation over the phone, and Jenny forbidden to text about it, I decided to find the information another way. Still holding my phone after finishing the call, I quickly typed out a message to Sage:

> What's the cause of death?

She texted back:

> You know I'm the forensic photographer, not the coroner?

I replied:

> But you know, don't you?

> Looks like blunt force trauma to the back of the head.

I didn't want to know anything else. I wasn't getting involved this time. This wasn't my crime to solve. My relationship with Dexter was better than ever and I planned to keep it on track by not interfering with a police investigation...*again*. Even if Jenny decided to record a podcast series on the murder, I wanted no part of it.

I called my aunt and filled her in, and tried to console her as best I could.

"I was just trying to help him. That's why I checked him in to the hospital." She took a deep, shuttery breath. "I'm coming over." She hung up.

Sage texted me:

> I emailed you the crime scene photos for your murder board.

> Hey, just letting you know I can't help you set up the murder board tonight.

I texted back:

> There will not be a murder board. I'm sitting this one out.

Sage:

> Oh. Well, I've got to write an article about the town hall meeting for the paper.

Me:

> That's actually perfect. The town could use a clear story about what's happening. Good luck with it!

Sage:

> Thanks! Let me know if you need anything later.

Me:

Will do. ☺

Fifteen minutes later, I heard Jenny and the college students in the hallway outside my apartment.

"Do you think Harper will have the murder board set up?" Ryan asked.

"I can't believe Cassy saw a dead body," Ethan added.

Aunt Mary interrupted their conversation. "There's not going to be a murder investigation. Now, if you don't mind, I'd like to talk to Harper."

"Aunt Mary, what do you mean?" Jenny asked.

I opened the door to ask them to bring the discussion inside. Before I could say a word, Rory shot down the stairs again in a flurry of amber colored fur. And Mary said, "Dexter said there is no murder. It was an accidental death."

I didn't follow Rory. Jake offered to walk him again. So after grabbing the leash, all three male co-eds opted for a walk in the frigid temperatures rather than comfort a grieving fifty-something aunt.

Aunt Mary sat on the sectional weeping while I made her a cup of hot chocolate. Jenny sat next to her, not knowing what to say.

I didn't know why Aunt Mary was so upset. I mean, I know Elmer was dead and he was a sweet man, but I saw and interacted with him more frequently than she did. He was one of The Classics and I'm sure he would be the topic of conversation the next day. They'd have questions for me. Stories to share.

I set a steaming mug of hot chocolate in front of her and one in front of Jenny and joined her on the sectional. "Tell me about it," I said, like she used to say to me when I was a little girl.

"He was so upset when I took him to the hospital. He thought I was dropping him off at the university to give a lecture on some bird." She grabbed a tissue from the box and dabbed her eyes. "You should have seen his face when the nurse led him away. She had to get an orderly to help him. He was still yelling about a bird and getting his research."

"It's not your fault he's dead," Jenny said while patting her awkwardly on the back.

I handed her another tissue. "She's right, Aunt Mary. Elmer was sick, and you were the only one willing to step out of your comfort zone and help him."

"Could I speak to you for a moment in private?" Jenny whispered behind Aunt Mary's back as she blew her nose loudly.

I stood and said, "We'll be right back."

Because my apartment was so open, having a private conversation was not an easy feat to manage. I led Jenny to the laundry room, where I'd just returned the vacuum cleaner, and shut the door. The drying rack with my hiking pants, drying out from today's lecture, filled most of the space.

Jenny leaned against the dryer and pushed the button to start it. "I don't want your aunt to hear. But you need to know. Sage doesn't agree with the accidental death ruling. She said she thinks someone attacked him and he fell and hit his head."

"What does Dexter say?"

"I don't know. We weren't allowed to stay and chat."

"What should we do?"

"I think we need a murder board. We need to solve this thing."

I thought about my aunt sitting on the couch sipping hot chocolate and blaming herself for Elmer's death. Then a shadowy memory popped out of an old file tucked away in my memory. Her father had suffered a heart attack and hit his head when she confronted him about abusing her and my mother. This was a trigger for her. I studied the shelf of laundry detergent and cleaners. There weren't many things I could do for Aunt Mary after all she'd done for me. Raising me. Homeschooling me. She put her entire life on hold to care for me through the darkest moments of my panic attacks and agoraphobia. If I could clean this up for her by finding the real killer and ease her conscience, I was going to do it.

"Let's set up the murder board," I replied.

CHAPTER 6
CRIMECASTER AND CHRISTMAS TREE CONSPIRACIES

JAKE AND RYAN carried my plotting-turned-murder board down from my office. Ethan grabbed the easel and moved it down. Rory assisted by weaving around their legs while they descended the stairs.

My phone buzzed. A text from Zoe.

I'm locking up. See you tomorrow.

The Cozy Corner had closed at seven, but Zoe had come back after lock up because she wanted to clean some of the machinery and Rosy, the bookkeeper, wanted to catch up on some accounting work.

Nine o'clock found my apartment buzzing with excitement and grief. Aunt Mary had gone home after I promised her I would find out who killed Elmer.

I set up the murder board and handed Jake my laptop. "Sage sent me the photos from the crime scene in an email. Can you print them?"

"What's your password?" he asked as he set it down on the dining table.

"Do you really need it?" I asked.

"No, but wouldn't you rather me save my hacking skills for other tasks?" He pushed his glasses up on his nose before adding, "Is there coffee?"

I leaned over and typed my password in and opened my email account.

"I can make some coffee," Cassy offered.

Who was this girl? Not the feminist agenda spouting student I'd met last semester. I was going to find out, but this wasn't the time.

I ran upstairs to my office and stood by the printer, ready to catch the photos it spewed out. Rory followed me and settled down on her giant mustard pillow.

"It's not bedtime Rory," I said. "It's going to be a long night." She ignored me and put her head down. The printer hummed to life and spit out exactly fifty-five photos. Some of which were not from the crime scene.

I shuffled through the last set. Before I finished, Jake joined me, huffing from his jog up the stairs. "Jenny suggested we print some photos of suspects."

Cara. Fiona. Danny. Dr. Dennis. Edgar. I shuffled through some more. "Jenny," I yelled down the stairs, "this is half the town!"

"And...." she yelled back up.

Jake interrupted, "Robin is getting us some food from The Sandwich Shop before it closes at ten and she needs your order."

I grabbed a floral folder from my desk and stuffed the photos in.

"I knew you were old school," Jake said with a grin.

"I'll take a turkey and cranberry wrap *again*. Oh, and tell Cassy to go raid the day-old baked goods in the cafe." Sometimes eating the same food made me feel less overwhelmed. It helped me avoid decision fatigue.

"Cassy?" Jake looked puzzled. "She's going to say, 'It's not the 1950s anymore, you know.'"

"Then," I poked him in the shoulder with the folder, "why don't you go help her and prove to her you can do domestic tasks too? Get the mugs out. Grab the creamer."

"I don't know where any of that stuff is..." he said, as his eyes darted around the room in a panic.

Was that sweat beading on his forehead?

"Same place they've always been. You'll figure it out. Or you could ask her."

With a folder and a box of magnets in hand, I descended the stairs, following Jake, who trudged ahead with his head lowered like a scolded puppy. At the bottom, Robin was waiting, arms crossed and eyebrows raised. "Well?"

Jake shot her a quick scowl. "Well, what?"

Gosh, you'd think I'd taken Jake's laptop away and banned him from electronics instead of asking him to grab coffee supplies and baked goods.

"Cranberry and turkey wrap," I answered for him, shifting the box under my arm.

Robin nodded briskly. "Thank you. I'll put in our order and have it delivered." She turned on her heel, already reaching for her phone.

I watched him as he moved toward the kitchen like

a sloth. Cassy was humming behind the counter, loading grounds into the filter basket.

Jenny cut off my viewing by stepping in front of me. "Crime scene photos?" She grabbed the folder out of my hand.

I turned and joined her, Ethan and Ryan at the board. "We're going to have to eliminate some of these townspeople as suspects before we build the board."

"Are those magnets?" Ryan asked, his curiosity evident as he reached out to touch the box.

"Yes, they're special murder magic magnets," Jenny replied, a mischievous laugh escaping her lips.

"Can I put something on the board?" Ethan chimed in, his eyes already darting toward the empty space on the board.

A loud crash interrupted us. I turned just in time to see a mug sail through mid air before Cassy reached out and caught it by the handle.

"See I'm no good at this domestic stuff," Jake said as he stomped out of the kitchen.

"Broom and dustpan are in the laundry room," Cassy called after him.

With the kitchen crisis under control, I turned back to the murder board. I'd address the domestic stuff with Jake later.

"How's your handwriting, Ethan?"

"Pretty good."

"Why don't you write 'Elmer's Murder' and the date across the top?"

While Ethan wrote with the dry erase marker, I suggested we go through the suspect photos. I plopped down on the floor. Robin, Jenny, and Ryan joined me.

"Bea the baker? Really, Jenny?"

"Okay, don't put her on the board." She put Bea's photo in the discard pile.

"We're going down to get some goodies," Cassy said with her hand on the doorknob. "We'll grab the food order too. If it arrives, text me, Robin."

I stifled a chuckle as Jake followed Cassy out the door, his shoulders slumped like a kid being dragged to the principal's office.

When he mouthed, "My time could be better spent on the computer," I had to bite my lip to keep from laughing outright. Snickerdoodles clearly weren't his idea of a worthy mission.

After sorting through a stack of non-suspects, we finally got to the photos of actual suspects.

I handed a stack of papers to Ryan and Robin, asking them to label and hang them on the right side of the board. Meanwhile, Jenny, Ethan, and I worked on the left side, arranging crime scene photos and leaving space for a timeline.

Jake and Cassy returned after the food arrived, so we took a break to eat and fuel ourselves with coffee for the next stage of the investigation. Now it was time to discuss the next stage—research and timelines and interview assignments.

As I took a sip of my coffee, letting the warmth seep through me, I volunteered, "I'll talk to The Classics in the morning."

Jenny leaned forward, drumming her fingers lightly on the table. "I'll talk to Sage and see if she knows anything."

"Who will talk to Danny?" I asked, glancing around.

"I will," Cassy jumped in, her voice a little too eager as she straightened up in her chair.

"I'll talk to our other classmates," Ryan said with a shrug. "They're not on the board, of course, but news travels." He tapped his pen against the edge of his notebook.

"That leaves Fiona, Lila, Cara, Anora..." I trailed off, my gaze drifting to the window. "I guess all the campers."

Ethan scratched his head, his brow furrowing in thought. "We don't have class at Christmas Tree Forest until next week."

"Well, Harper has winter camping dates there with Detective Dexter," Jenny said, grinning mischievously as she lobbed a throw pillow at my head.

I caught it just in time, frowning. "I don't want him to know I'm investigating."

Jenny's grin widened. "Then you'll have to be a real sleuth," she teased, arching an eyebrow.

With our bellies full, fueled by caffeine, sugar, and curiosity, we began to piece together a timeline and possible motives.

"Why would anyone want Elmer dead?" Jenny asked, tapping a dry erase marker on the murder board beneath his photo. "Did he have money?" She pointed the marker at Jake. "Can you find out?"

"According to my aunt, he never married," I added.

For the next hour, we talked and ended up nowhere. At 11 p.m., I yawned and suggested we call it a day. Tomorrow the main agenda would be interviewing anyone and everyone in the town for more information on Elmer and possible reasons someone would want him dead.

Cassy helped me clean again. Jenny lingered to give her a ride home. Ethan, Ryan, Robin, and Jake went ahead, but not before loading up white paper bags with left-over baked goods for the road.

"Are you going to do a podcast series on this?" Cassy asked as she picked coffee mugs off the counter and loaded them in the sink.

I rinsed them, so my back was turned to Jenny. I was curious to hear her response. There was none. I set the sudsy mug down and turned.

Jenny studied my face before replying. While she inspected me for clues, I realized she hadn't released a new series since the College Co-ed Murders.

"I … don't… want to be responsible for more murders."

"I hardly think that there is a serial killer out there killing retired professors who struggle with dementia," I reassured her and then realized how ridiculous that sounded.

She laughed a nervous laugh and slapped the counter. "Do *you* think I should cover this case on Crimecaster?"

"I do. I think Elmer deserves it." I had other reasons for wanting her to record a series, but first and foremost, I wanted Elmer's killer to be brought to justice.

"Hey Harper, do you think Elmer's murder has anything to do with the commercial development of Christmas Tree Forest?" Cassy asked.

CHAPTER 7
STORMY NIGHTS AND STARTLING NEWS

"CASSY, I think you're onto something," Jenny said, as she typed on her phone. "I'm writing some notes for the first episode."

Cassy jumped up and down, flinging the dish towel around and hitting me in the face. "I'm good at something!"

I stepped back, removing myself from the towel-flinging danger zone, and thought two things. One, Jenny really wanted to record a new series. She was afraid that talking about murder caused them. Two, I suspected Cassy was trapped by a deeply rooted limiting belief, one powerful enough to drastically alter her behavior. Someone must have said something to her that triggered a memory or thought.

"Let's get going Cassy, so Miss Marple here can get some sleep."

In response to Jenny's statement, Cassy folded and hung up the dish towel.

"How are you at typing on a phone and pushing the record button?"

Jenny asked.

"Consider me your secretary," Cassy said, taking the phone from Jenny's hand. They grabbed their outerwear and said a quick "goodbye" while I held open the door to the apartment.

Jenny stopped on the threshold. "I'll arm the building."

"Thank you," I said.

"Now first of all, let's go over everything that happened at the town hall meeting. Let's...." Jenny's muffled voice continued as they descended the stairs.

Jenny lived with my aunt and had claimed my childhood bedroom. When she first came to town from New York City shortly after the death of her mother, she had needed a place to stay. My aunt, a realtor and interior designer, had offered to help her find a place. She had spent her first night in town in my old room, and she'd been there ever since. She'd become part of the family. The longer she lived in Evergreen Heights, the more her tough exterior melted, like the hard candy coating on an ice cream cone on a hot day.

I stopped musing and looked around my apartment. Sparkling clean. Nothing for me to do. When I had people over, especially my ever-expanding group of students, I spent the time after they left cleaning and thinking. Although Jenny cleared out of here for me to sleep, I couldn't sleep, thinking Elmer's killer was out there, and the clock was ticking to him getting away with it.

I pulled out a FlexiStride Ultra collapsible treadmill

from underneath my sectional. A gift from my toned and lean, sophisticated Mother, who quoted something her private trainer told her, "Sitting is the new smoking." I'm sure Mother had told her about her poor, broken agoraphobic daughter who didn't get enough exercise, which wasn't true. Number one, I owned a cafe and bookstore in a four story building and logged more than the recommended ten thousand steps inside. Number two, I hiked now with my friend Gabrielle or Dexter. I owned an ebike which got me around town, but it remained parked in the storage room during the winter months.

Regardless of all of the above, I was grateful for the treadmill. It allowed me to walk and think inside my apartment. I pulled the treadmill close to the murder board and hopped on. Jenny had taught me the power of recording my thoughts. I pulled my phone out of my pocket and opened the voice recorder app.

"Who wanted Elmer dead?

"What did this have to do with the commercialization of Christmas Tree Forest?"

Thirty minutes of walking and three hundred questions later, I had zero answers, just more questions. I stepped off the treadmill, slid it back under the sectional, and headed upstairs for a long soak in the tub. It was nearly midnight when I climbed into bed. A 5:30 writing time was going to feel a lot earlier than normal.

———

My writing time flew by with plenty of ideas for plot twists and red herrings in my current novel. When it was time for story hour, I was dressed in a forest green corduroy dress and mustard yellow Doc Martens. I thought the dress was a fitting tribute to Elmer.

Rory was already downstairs in the cafe, having been walked by Zoe before she picked up the baked goods from Bea's Bakery across the street. Bea kept a stash of dog biscuits for Rory, who had probably had more than one, and was now napping on her giant pillow in the corner of the cafe.

I bounded down the stairs, a surprising burst of energy carrying me despite my lack of sleep. Excitement buzzed under the surface—tonight I had another winter camping date with Dexter, and I was saving all my time outdoors for that. Last night, he hadn't texted, but I told myself it was because he was busy with the case. Still, I couldn't help the flicker of doubt wondering if something else had kept him away. *Wait, didn't he say accidental death?* I pulled out my phone to text him as I entered the cafe.

"Here's your Double Espresso, Boss," Zoe yelled.

Theo and Dominic sat at the counter munching on muffins. No powdered donut holes today. Clare and Ashley were busy cutting out mitten shapes. I grabbed my Double Espresso and perused the room. Something was missing. *Someone* was missing.

"Where are Audrey and Peregrine?" I asked.

"Great job, Boss. It only took you a minute to notice. You should write mysteries." Zoe slapped the counter with a wet dish towel and laughed at her own joke.

"Clare's sister is in town and with all the stuff going

on," she scanned the room with wide eyes before she continued, "we didn't know if Dr. Dennis would be here today."

"He helps a lot with those two," Clare explained. "My sister offered to watch them, so we took her up on it at the last minute."

"It's going to be a lot quieter in here," Zoe added as she delivered two steaming lattes to the table.

"Not if you don't stop talking," I said playfully.

"You're funny," Zoe said.

"So, the professor's death? Elmer?" Ashley set down the scissors and picked up her drink. "It was accidental?"

"No, I don't think so." Zoe hadn't moved from the table, instead she picked up a mitten template and traced another one.

"Why don't you think so?" Ashley asked. "I mean, the town has just gotten over the serial killer thing." She gripped her coffee until her knuckles turned the same white as the froth on her Peppermint Latte.

"Yes, why don't you think it was accidental?" I asked Zoe, with my hand on my hip. "When did you become the sleuth?"

"Oh, I'm not a sleuth. That's your job…"

"And?"

"Well, Jenny got the code wrong last night when she was arming the building. Sixty seconds before the alarm sounded, she called me and I gave her the correct code." She reached for the scissors and snipped out a mitten.

"What does that have to do with Elmer's death?" Ashely asked as she grabbed the mitten template.

"If Jenny Murder is at Harper's apartment arming the building after eleven p.m., that means a few things. There's a new murder board set up there in Harper's apartment."

"Is that true, Harper?" Clare asked.

I hesitated, glancing at Theo and Dominic, who were now running around the tables "sliming" each other with their slime blowers.

"Yes."

"What's the second thing?" Ashley asked as she cut out a mitten.

"Jenny Murder is planning to do a podcast series on Crimecaster Podcast," she said triumphantly as she slammed another mitten on the table.

"Is that true?" Ashley leaned in, her eyes wide with curiosity.

I nodded, glancing around as if to keep the information contained. "Yes, but let's keep that under wraps for this morning."

Zoe rolled her eyes, crossing her arms with a smirk. "Too late, Boss. She's dropping an episode as we speak."

I raised an eyebrow, studying her. "Are you more of a sleuth than I realized, or just glued to social media for your intel?"

"Both," she said. She twirled and hummed the theme song from *Mission Impossible* as she danced back to the cafe counter.

The front door opened and Dr. Dennis, followed by a few regulars and story hour kiddos, entered with a blast of winter air. "It's coming down hard," he said as he removed his wool coat and shook it out on the rubber doormat.

The movement at the door woke Rory, and he raced over to investigate. By investigate, I mean wagging his tail while sniffing the pile of mittens and snow gear that the moms were removing from their children.

Zoe got my attention by throwing a towel at my head. I took the not-too-subtle hint and joined the Moms at the door, sopping up the melting puddles of snow.

"Come on in and get warm," I said. "Don't worry about the snow. It's easy enough to clean up."

Clare and Ashley took charge of the kids, while Zoe got busy filling drink orders.

After sopping up the water, I took the towel behind the counter and dumped it in a bin. Then I went to check on story hour.

Ashley handed me the pile of construction paper mittens. "Can you organize the craft?"

While Clare and Ashey got the kids seated on cushions in the bookstore, I finished organizing the craft.

"*The Mitten* by Jan Brett," Dr. Dennis's voice resounded, deep and powerful.

I guess I wouldn't be interviewing him this morning. Not that he was a suspect. Scratch that. He was here, helping with story hour because he'd been a suspect in the College Co-ed Killer Case. He hadn't actually kidnapped anyone. But he'd drugged Simone and set it up to look like a kidnapping. Even though Simone, the student, hadn't filed charges, the judge had assigned community service. Turns out, the law doesn't look too kindly on fake kidnappings even if the culprit is a doctor of psychiatry trying to save the community from more harm.

I gathered the mittens, glue sticks, and pompoms. Inside Ashley's bag I found stickers of the animals who'd crawled in the mittens. What a cute craft. The kiddos were meant to glue the pompoms on the giant mitten and then stick the animals on the mitten. Easy-peasy and not messy compared to yesterday's powdered donut hole disaster.

After the story, I helped with the craft.

"Once there was a boy named Nicki who wanted his new mittens made from wool as white as snow," Dominic quoted as he left the craft table and ran to look out the window.

"It's a whiteout," Theo yelled.

"I think we should end the story hour early," I suggested.

Zoe waved her phone and said, "You're right, this is just the tip of the winter storm."

As Ashley and Clare packed up individual craft bags, Zoe and I did the same with the snacks.

Dr. Dennis entertained the kids by having them re-enact the story as if each of them was an animal crawling in a mitten. He was the bear.

"The bear, tickled by the mouse's whiskers, gave an enormous sneeze. Aaaaa-aaaaa-aaaaa-ca-chew! The force of the sneeze shot the mitten up into the sky, and scattered the animals in all directions," he recited and the kids scattered, laughing and falling over top of each other.

Ten minutes later, the cafe was empty except for Zoe, Rory, and I. A snowplow sped by, covering the sidewalk in front of the Cozy Corner with a drift, blocking the door.

"I don't think The Classics are coming in today," I said to Rory.

"I don't think anyone is coming in today," Zoe answered for him as she stacked up Ashley's and Clare's latte mugs.

"Do you want to go home?" I asked, eyeing the storm outside.

"Nah, I'll stay. We might get some people stranded who need a hot cup of coffee or hot chocolate."

"Thank you," I replied.

I helped her clean up and wipe tables before settling down with a Double Espresso at the counter.

I took a sip of my brew and sighed. All my plans for the day, including my date with Dexter, rose like the steam of my coffee and dissipated into thin air. I shifted on my seat.

"Did Jenny release her episode this morning?"

"I'll check." She pulled her phone out of her apron pocket. "Yep. Should we listen?"

The wind howled as I nodded yes.

She pushed play.

Episode 101: Mystery in Christmas Tree Forest
Jenny Murder:

"Elmer Rockwoods's death was ruled an accident, but something doesn't sit right with me—and I'm not the only one raising eyebrows. This retired forestry professor spent decades protecting Christmas Tree Forest, so why would he suddenly have a fatal

'accident' just as Lila Weston shows up with big plans to commercialize the land?

"Was Elmer standing in the way of a lucrative deal, or did he know too much about what was really going on? I think it's time we start asking the tough questions, because I'm not convinced Elmer just happened to die at the most convenient time for some people."

After listening to the podcast, Zoe and I spent the whole day intermittently talking about the case and serving a few customers who were stranded by the storm. Many of them were waiting for the snowplow to take another pass down the street so they could go home.

At five o'clock, as the snowstorm intensified, we decided to close the Cozy Corner. The wind whipped against the windows, rattling the panes and carrying a sharp chill that nipped at our cheeks. The air smelled crisp and icy, tinged with the faint scent of pine from the wreath on the door. Flurries swirled in the glow of the streetlights outside, while the warmth of freshly brewed coffee lingered in the air. Zoe turned on the closed signs and locked the door, leaving the storm's icy breath outside.

As soon as she flipped the lock, a face pressed up against the glass, centered in the evergreen wreath. We both jumped. All the talk about murderers triggered a chill up our spines.

"Let me in," Sage mouthed. "I have news about the case."

Jenny's head bobbed behind her, floating in the air like the headless horseman. "Let us in!"

CHAPTER 8
PRACTICING WISDOM AND UNCOVERING CLUES

JENNY AND SAGE burst through the door, trailing a gust of frigid air that instantly prickled my skin with goosebumps. A flurry of snow swept in behind them. The sharp scent of winter followed, a damp, earthy crispness of freshly fallen snow. Their cheeks were flushed red from the cold, and their boots left wet prints that squeaked against the wooden floor. As they shook off the snow from their coats, puddles formed on the floor.

"What are you two doing out there? There's a winter weather advisory and everyone is asked to stay indoors," I chided.

"We were at my studio all day and couldn't drive home, so we came here." That made sense. Sage's studio was five blocks away.

"Wouldn't it have been safer to stay there?" Zoe asked.

"Yes, it would have," Jenny answered. She hung her dripping leather jacket on a hook. "But Sage doesn't have baked goods, lattes, and an apartment to camp out in."

"True," Zoe said. "I'll get the mop vac. These puddles are more than a towel can handle."

As I gathered hats, scarves, and gloves, I said, "I'll throw these in the dryer. Zoe can fire up the machines and make you some hot drinks."

"I have two words," Zoe said as she danced behind the cafe counter and grabbed the mop vac. "Slumber party."

"I thought we could have a murder mystery party," Jenny said. As I took the first steps to my apartment, I heard what sounded like hands slapping. Jenny and Zoe must be high fiving each other.

"We listened to your first episode of the *Mystery in Christmas Tree Forest* series."

Their voices faded as I opened my apartment. I flipped on the lights and went directly to the laundry room. As I opened the dryer, my phone buzzed. I pulled it out of my pocket. A text from Dexter:

> Sorry we have to cancel our date. Do you mind if I stop by?

Stop by? What was he doing out in the middle of this storm?

I didn't answer immediately, and he texted again:

> I'm here. Zoe let me in.

Talk about not giving a girl time to think. After setting the timer on the dryer and pushing start, I ran out into the living room. My first thought was how to cover the murder board. Did I get a spare sheet? Who was I kidding? Knowing Zoe, not only had she talked about my murder board and my thoughts on Elmer's death, she probably told him all about my murder meeting last night. Not to mention Jenny... I ran for the door in my apartment and ran down the stairs without taking the time to shut the door.

When I entered the cafe, Jenny was interviewing Dexter while Zoe pressed espresso for drinks.

Jenny had placed her mic in the center of a table. How did she manage that so quickly?

"Who do you think had a motive to kill Elmer?"

"Yes, Detective. Harper has a long list on her murder board," Zoe chimed in.

Dexter removed his coat and scarf and moved away from the puddle he'd created on the floor. "Sage, I thought we ruled this an accident." He hung his coat and scarf on a hook.

"I'll grab the mop vac," I squeaked and ran behind the counter.

Sage stood and took a defensive pose, both hands on her hips. "I've changed my mind after examining the crime scene photos."

"And just when did you change your mind?"

"Right before I came here. I've been busy writing a story about the snowstorm today," Sage said. She ruffled her blonde pixie hair, freeing the last bits of water droplets.

Dexter put an arm out to stop me as I rounded the counter with mop vac in hand. "But you put together a murder board and had, what did you call it, Zoe? A Murder Club meeting."

I set the mop vac on the floor and waited as he pivoted and addressed Jenny. "And you, you released the first in a podcast series on Elmer's alleged murder."

"Oh no, not alleged. The podcast assumes it is murder," Zoe said before firing up the espresso machine, essentially blocking her from hearing what Dexter said next.

You're not helping us, Zoe, I thought. *You're making it worse.*

"I've got to clean this up before..." I pushed the button on the mop vac and sucked up the puddle vigorously and continued to mop all the way to the door.

I busied myself with emptying the water tank in the supply room, avoiding the scolding that was sure to come. As I watched the gray water swirl around the drain, I imagined my relationship with Dexter going down the drain as well.

"Hey," he said from behind me. "I came in here so we could talk alone."

"Okay, talk," I said as I clicked the water tank back into the mop vac with a little too much force.

"What are you doing?"

"I'm putting the mop vac away." I replied.

"I mean, why are you investigating this and involving a bunch of college students?"

"What do you mean *involving?*"

"I'm the detective."

"I teach a class on murder."

"You teach a creative writing class."

"About murder."

"And Jenny. Are you helping her put this podcast on? You're going to scare the whole town."

"I'm not scaring the whole town. Someone murdered Elmer. I didn't murder him."

"What?"

"You should do your job and catch the murderer. Not let some college kids who start a murder club and a woman who teaches creative writing do it for you."

"Are you serious?"

"I am. Did you ever think Elmer's murder had something to do with Lila Weston and her plan to commercialize Christmas Tree Forest?"

I stomped out of the utility room, leaving him standing at the utility sink.

"So Boss, I have everyone's orders but yours."

"I don't want anything. I'm going upstairs. Come on Rory." Rory stood and stretched in a downward facing dog before slowly dragging his back legs across the floor. So much for a dramatic exit.

"I'll take mine to go," Dexter said.

The wind outside howled in disagreement, and a blast of snow hit the front door.

"I don't think you're going anywhere, Detective Dexter," Sage said with the emphasis on his name.

Dexter was now trapped in a building with four women who thought Elmer had been murdered. He might be next. At least with words.

I left him alone with three of the women. Once inside my apartment, I shut the door. I plopped a pod in the Keurig and waited as it hissed and pushed the brew into the mug with an inscription "I'm always write."

I moved to the living room and studied the murder board.

If Elmer's murder did have something to do with Christmas Tree Forest and Coldwater Corp, then Lila Weston was the first person I should question. There was no use in trying to go in-person tonight, or at least until midmorning tomorrow, when and if they got the roads cleared.

I grabbed a remote and clicked my gas fireplace on. It instantly felt warmer. I wrapped a blanket around me and sat on the sectional. Rory camped out in front of the fire, probably hoping some marshmallows would follow. Then I thought of a few nights ago when I'd burned my marshmallow and what a good time I'd had with Dexter. Had our relationship literally gone down the drain like the gray dirty water?

I was still learning how to navigate healthy relation-ships, and since dating Dexter was my first romantic relationship ever, I'd made plenty of mistakes. But was I making one this time? I'm pretty sure belittling your girlfriend wasn't a good practice. Isn't that what my dad did that caused a gaping wound and rift between us? He called my bookstore "little" and didn't view my writing books as a career, instead as a hobby until I took over his business. His business required travel all over the world and I could barely leave my building for more than two hours, which put me in the "broken" category in his eyes. I just needed to pull myself together and meet his expectations—like he thought being autistic and agoraphobic was a choice I had made.

Now here was Dexter, maintaining the same

mantras. Not good enough. *Little* class. Who are you to solve a murder? A fiery serpent raised up in the bowels of my belly, like a Balrog. I wasn't going to sit here alone in my little anything. I planned on solving Elmer's murder. I stood and threw the blanket aside. I pulled out my phone and texted Jake:

> Can you find out where Lila Weston is staying?

He texted back:

> Yes.

A minute later, a second text from Jake:

> Can Robin, Cassy, and I come over? We're stuck at the library and it's closing.

Five minutes later, the building felt as if it were bursting at the seams. I struggled with whether I should go downstairs and let them in, or leave them to their fate.

"Hey, can I come in?" Dexter asked as he knocked lightly on the door.

I texted Zoe and let her know the college students were coming before answering the door.

"I'm sorry," he said when I opened the door.

I didn't answer. To me, it was more important to know why he was sorry, not just that he was. I'd heard so many "I'm sorrys" in my lifetime without any backbone or real repentance behind them.

Rory greeted him by licking Dexter's hands and running around the dining room table.

I backed up so he could enter and continue his apology.

"I talked to Sage. She thinks it is murder. Jenny too and she's…"

I bit my tongue. I wanted to say "why did you need someone else to say it was murder?" But that wasn't really fair, because Sage and Jenny were experts on the subject of murder. I was an expert on writing about murder. Pastor Dr. Samuel Whitaker had been preaching a series on relational intelligence. I was trying to get better at not judging a person's motives based on their words. I recalled what I'd written in my notes from his last sermon:

"Relational intelligence is about more than just knowing how to interact with others; it's about understanding the heart behind the interaction. It means listening deeply, showing empathy, and being intentional in our connections. Jesus modeled this for us by meeting people where they were and understanding their needs before offering help or advice. When we prioritize relational intelligence, we build trust, foster deeper relationships, and reflect God's love in our everyday lives."

I was quick to pounce on people with my words when they didn't use the exact words I thought they should or if I didn't think about the fact that they may have a motive. I was still holding the door open, thinking, when I realized Dexter hadn't finished his sentence or apology.

Dexter had moved across the room and was studying the murder board. "Sage is right, you know."

Before I could answer, Robin, Jake, and Cassy practically fell through the door in a heap of backpacks and, with them, the distinct smell of a bacon avocado burger.

"We brought dinner," Robin said, holding up two paper bags as proof.

"Yes, The Grill was closing early too, and we got in an order just in time."

Ethan and Ryan pulled up the rear. "Oh, yeah, we brought Ryan and Ethan. They were stuck in the library with us all day too."

"Is that Detective Dexter? Is he helping us with the murder board?"

Ethan asked excitedly as he pumped his arms up in the air.

"Harper's dating him," Cassy said as she smacked him in the shoulder. There's the Cassy I know and love.

"To answer your question, young man, yes, I'm helping with the murder board."

My phone buzzed. I pulled it out of my dress pocket. Zoe:

> I got everyone's drink orders but yours.
> Is it safe to come up?

I texted back:

> I'll take a Double Espresso and bring all
> the baked goods, Jenny and Sage too.

The ten of us spread out over the dining room, living room, and kitchen, munching on burgers and chatting. Evergreen Heights was no stranger to winter storms. The early snow was one reason the Christmas Tree Forest Christmas Fair was a huge hit for the tri-state area. We were guaranteed to have snow by Thanksgiving. And often the snow hung out through March, or at least blew its last stormy breath in the middle of March. A few odd storms hit in May, but we were used to it. When a storm of this magnitude blocked the roads in and out of town, the college canceled classes for the day and the businesses tried to stay open as long as possible to serve the residents.

I split my burger with Dexter since the students hadn't expected him and hadn't brought food for him. Although he hadn't finished his apology, it felt good to sit and eat with him without the dark storm clouds of anger hanging over us.

Everyone talked about the weather for the first ten minutes. We might be used to the weather, but this was Ryan, Ethan, Jenny, and Dexter's first winter here.

Zoe and Sage were full of stories about being trapped in a restaurant or the snow, and neighbors or friends digging them out.

"What about you Harper? Do you have a snow story?" Ethan asked.

Robin elbowed him in the side.

"What the heck?" he said.

"I spent a lot of time at her house during storms," Sage offered, trying to cover my whatever-you-call-them. Panic attacks. Episodes. Agoraphobia.

"No, it's fine, Sage. I don't mind telling the truth."

"What truth?" Ethan asked.

"Most of my childhood I didn't leave the home. I'm agoraphobic."

You could have heard a crispy sweet potato fry drop.

"You're afraid of spiders?" Ryan asked, joining the conversation.

Robin chuckled before saying, "that's arachnophobia."

"Agoraphobia is like being held hostage by your own mind, convincing you that ordinary places are dangerous. It's not just fear—it's the nagging dread of losing control in spaces where you can't easily escape. For someone like me, who loves the cozy refuge of a bookstore, it's ironic. Words take me anywhere, but sometimes it's a struggle to step outside my own door," I explained.

"Wow..." Ryan and Ethan both were rendered speechless.

Cassy jumped up to clean up again, and I joined her as everyone else grabbed cookies and moved to the murder board.

As we gathered foil burger wrappers and greasy napkins, I asked, "Why this sudden interest in domestic tasks?"

"Like cleaning?" she asked. "Well, I kind of like a guy." She crumpled up a paper bag and threw it in the trash can.

I uttered a short prayer. *Please don't let it be man-bun Danny.*

"Is it Danny?"

"Who?"

"The camper who helped at the lecture on Hemlock Trail."

She laughed. "Harper, that guy is easy on the eyes." She tapped her head. "But deficient on, what does Poirot say, the little gray cells?"

"So the guy you like has lots of little gray cells?"

I scanned the room. Jake had set up his laptop on the coffee table and while everyone else discussed the crime scene photos, he tapped away, ignoring the comments in excited voices like "is that blood?" "How did the murderer enter?"

"Jake," I said.

"I knew you'd figure it out."

"But why do you suddenly need to do household chores? What happened to your liberated 'I'm not getting the coffee because this is not the 1950s' soapbox?" I grabbed the sponge and squirted some winter pine cleaner on the counter.

"I'm not changing my belief. I'm changing my behavior to suit his needs."

I scrubbed at a honey barbecue stain vigorously and waited for her to continue.

She stopped cleaning and leaned her hip against the counter. "Ever since Pastor Sam started his series on relational intelligence, I realized how reactionary I am to others. I'm acting on my limiting beliefs instead of their felt-needs."

"That's pretty profound."

"I'm just reciting the sermon. Those are Dr. Sam's words. I'm just trying to put them into practice, not just with Jake. With everyone."

"Isn't that changing who you are to suit the person?"

"No, according to Pastor Sam, your attitudes and behaviors are not who you are, they are what you do."

"So to accommodate Jake's lack of ability in the cleaning department, you're taking on more of those *tasks for* him?"

I paused and wrung out the sponge after rinsing the honey barbecue sauce out, watching it circle the drain. Earlier, I'd watched the gray water of the mop vac circle the drain and thought my relationship with Dexter was over because we'd had an argument. I'd let instinct win over wisdom. My instinct said to run and hide and quit if I felt threatened or belittled by someone else's words. Cassy was applying wisdom. Meeting her partner's needs.

I set the sponge on the wire rack. "Does he know?"

"That I like him or that I clean and prepare food?"

"Both."

"He knows I like him. Does he need to know the other?"

"Are you two helping solve this murder or not?" Jenny yelled.

Jake raised a hand in the air to signal for quiet. "You're going to want to see this, Detective Dexter."

CHAPTER 9
FAMILY TIES AND SUSPICIOUS LIES

DEXTER REACHED Jake and his laptop first, with everyone else following and crowding around him.

"Watch," Jake said as he flipped through some photos of Elmer's study. In the first photo, the desk was covered with photos, papers, files, and a laptop. In the following crime scene photos, the desk was clean.

Dexter grabbed the laptop and scrolled through them again, studying them while the rest of us stood waiting. "Where did you get these photos?"

"So it's weird. Elmer only has cameras inside his study." He took the laptop back and clicked another tab and scanned the study.

It felt like walking into a cozy forest retreat. The walls were lined with sturdy wooden shelves over-flowing with well-worn books on botany and forestry. A faded, forest-green armchair sat beside a window that overlooked the wooded backyard where Elmer no doubt spent countless hours observing the trees, but now was covered with frost. A large oak desk dominated one corner, shining as if someone had wiped it clean like a crime scene.

"How did you get access to his security camera?" Dexter demanded.

"You don't want to know," Robin and Cassy said in unison.

"Why doesn't he have cameras in other parts of his house?" Ryan asked.

"Good question," I replied. "And what was so valuable in his study that he had the one and only camera in there?"

"Oh, there's one more camera on the front porch." Jake added. "Want me to pull it up?"

"Can you pull it up for the night of the murder?" Dexter asked, taking a seat next to him on the sectional and leaning over the coffee table.

"Sure, give me a sec," Jake answered, plunking away. "Is there coffee?" he asked no one in particular.

"I'll grab you a cup," Cassy offered.

Cassy returned to the kitchen with Zoe, who suggested they make a large pot. I grabbed the dry erase markers and headed to the murder board.

I wrote:

Elmer had a camera in his study.

Followed by the question:

What was so valuable that he needed a camera there?

Robin, Jake, and Elmer joined me at the board.

"What could Elmer have had that was so valuable?" Ryan asked.

I turned to Robin. "You went to the town hall meeting. You are our eyewitness to what happened right before someone murdered Elmer."

"Well, I watched the stage most of the time, occasionally looking down to take notes—"

Sage interrupted with, "Here, take a seat." She'd hauled a few chairs from the dining room table.

Ethan and Ryan took a cue from her and grabbed the two other chairs that weren't occupied. I pulled an armchair over to the corner of the board.

"Let's go over everything from the beginning of the town hall meeting to when Elmer left. Leave nothing out." I stated.

I hopped out of my chair and drew a timeline on the board. With the words beginning and end and a line in between, not that I need that. It looked better that way.

"The mayor opened the meeting with an introduction and welcome."

I drew a stick figure of the mayor.

"What is that?" Sage asked, and laughed.

"It's the mayor," I said.

"Let me do the drawing," Robin offered. I slumped my shoulders forward in mock shame. I handed her a marker.

She drew a character head of the mayor in a few seconds flat.

"What was going on in the rest of the room? We couldn't see it. The Zoom camera was focused on the stage and podium," I asked.

"I've got this!" Jenny said. "I recorded the meeting."

"Why did you do that?"

"You predicted the murder?" Ethan asked. "That's freaky and sus."

"She didn't predict the murder. She records people all the time without their permission," Sage said, the old storm clouds between Sage and Jenny brewing.

"It's an occupational habit," Jenny said, flopping in the chair Ryan had just vacated. "The better question is, why didn't you record the meeting? Didn't you write a story for the paper about it?"

Sage's face turned the crimson color of a male cardinal. She swallowed before saying, "Yes, I did record it."

"Good, we have two recordings to listen to," I interjected, trying to smooth the wrinkles out of Sage and Jenny's relationship.

"We need more than just me at the board," Robin suggested.

"You're right, I'll join you." I stood up and held out a dry erase marker to Ethan. "You game?"

"As long as you promise not to draw anything," Robin elbowed me with her black sweater clad arm.

Jenny pushed play.

The audio crackled softly as Lila's voice came through, smooth and confident. "Hello everyone, thanks for welcoming me to your wonderful little town of Evergreen Heights." A pattering of light applause followed.

"What I'd like to do tonight is give you the vision I have for expanding the tourism at Christmas Tree Forest and boosting the economy of your town." There was a faint whirring sound as a screen dropped from the ceiling, followed by a brief rustle from the audience. "Now, if you look at the screen, you'll see Christmas Tree Forest with the pristine lake in the center."

There was a pause, and a few moments of silence stretched out, punctuated by the occasional cough or shuffle. Lila's voice came back on, calm and deliberate.

"In the literary world, we call this the dramatic pause," I explained.

A faint click could be heard, and then her voice continued, "Now, imagine this," as the next photo appeared.

The murmur of voices grew louder as the new image displayed. Lila's tone remained steady. "As you can see, we have plans for chalets and a condo surrounding the lake." A mixture of gasps and low whispers filled the background, some words indistinct, while others were clearer.

"That's our forest..." an older woman's voice said, barely audible. "Looks more like a ski resort."

A man's voice could be heard from closer to the microphone. "I don't like the sound of this. More traffic's gonna ruin Main Street."

Lila's tone grew more upbeat, though the tension in the room was palpable. "I know what some of you might be thinking," she continued, accompanied by another faint click as the slide changed. "But rest assured, this plan has been carefully designed to preserve the natural beauty of Christmas Tree Forest while providing new opportunities for the community."

The murmuring persisted, now joined by the sound of a chair creaking as someone rose. A man's voice, louder and more insistent, broke through. "What happens to all the hiking trails? The wildlife? You're talking about putting up chalets where folks have been camping for generations!"

Lila's reply was poised, with a hint of practiced patience. "Great question," she said. "We're planning to upgrade the existing trails to ensure a world-class experience for outdoor enthusiasts, attracting more visitors and boosting local businesses."

The background noise of voices rose again, making it clear that Lila's assurances hadn't quite settled the crowd. The recording captured a growing mix of skepticism and concern from the attendees.

"Do you recognize anyone's voices?" I asked.

"Wait, I haven't gotten to the good part," Jenny said. She pushed play again.

The audio recording crackled with background noise before a voice rang out, a bit muffled but firm: "You can't do that!"

There was a brief pause, then Dexter's voice came in, calm but authoritative. "Let's let Mrs. Weston finish her presentation."

"Yes, I'll reserve time for a Q and A at the end," Lila responded, her tone professional. A faint rustle of fabric could be heard as she flipped her ponytail.

But the voice persisted, growing louder. "I was supposed to give a lecture on the bird." The sound of hurried footsteps followed as Elmer shuffled up to the stage, papers rustling in his hands.

"Elmer," Lila said softly, but he was already at the podium, his voice unsteady yet determined. "You're a pretty lady, aren't ya?" Elmer began. "But I need to lecture my students on the Cerulean Warblers, so if you don't mind leaving the lecture hall…"

The audio captured a sigh of frustration from Lila. "Detective, if you could do your job?" Her voice was tight, frustration seeping through.

There was a scuffling sound, and instead of Dexter's voice, another figure seemed to intervene. Danny's voice was a low murmur, too soft for the mic to pick up, but whatever he said to Elmer, it seemed to calm him. The faint shuffling of feet could be heard as Elmer stepped down.

The recording then caught a faint whisper from Lila. "Thanks, son." Her tone softened, the tension momentarily diffused.

"Did Lila call Danny *son*?" I asked, frowning as the memory resurfaced. How could I have forgotten that? We'd talked about it while watching the Zoom town hall meeting.

"Yes, he's Lila's son," Jake replied, nodding.

Dexter leaned forward in his chair. "I've got the address for the Airbnb where Lila is staying," he said casually.

I threw up my hands. "Way to bury the lead, guys."

Sage crossed her arms, her brow furrowed. "What do those two have to do with Elmer's murder?"

"Lila, the corporate developer, and man-bun, outdoor-loving Danny?" I turned back to the whiteboard, scribbling furiously. "I think they could have a lot to do with it."

"You mean *fake* outdoorsman?" Dexter's voice dripped with skepticism.

I paused, the dry-erase marker hovering in midair. "You noticed?" I glanced at him.

"Of course I noticed," he replied, shrugging. "He's just a kid who needs friends."

"So he just happens to make those friends at Christmas Tree Forest?" Jenny chimed in, cocking an eyebrow.

"Sounds fishy to me," Sage's voice cut through. She bit her lip as if she were thinking about it.

"Me too." I capped the marker with a click.

Jenny leaned back in her chair, her expression serious. "I think we need to pay a visit to Lila and Danny as soon as the storm lets up."

CHAPTER 10

PARTNERS IN CRIME-SOLVING AND SOMETHING MORE

THE SNOWSTORM DIDN'T LET up for two more days. The plows ran as often as they could through the middle of town, creating ten to fifteen foot drifts on the sidewalks, making foot traffic impossible.

I spent the last day of the storm alone at the Cozy Corner with it closed. While it gave me time to work on my book, it made me realize how much I missed the kids at story hour, The Classics, my friends, and my new group of students.

Aunt Mary texted me exactly ten times the last day of the storm, making sure I had food, water, and heat. Plus, she was bored because the film crew was holed up in a hotel. Everything on the set had been halted. None of the crew could make it to the site. So the new kitchen cabinets sat in a warehouse on the edge of town. Aunt Mary lamented that it might be damp and they could get ruined.

I was fine. I had water, heat, and food. Aunt Mary had insisted I have a backup generator installed because Evergreen Heights was famous for these mammoth winter storms.

There was no news on the case of Elmer's murder. It felt as if we were in the middle of writing one of my novels. Once I had plotted it out and written the beginning, I would get excited and the words would flow like water from the tap. When I would get to the middle, it would slow to the flow of cold molasses. Or sometimes it would feel like I was trudging through the ten feet snowdrifts to get to the finish line.

We set up a Zoom coffee date so Aunt Mary could see me and we could chat face-to-face. I didn't bother to tame my curls or dress in real clothes for the meeting because I'd been working on writing my book. With the new teaching job at Evergreen University and my dating life, my writing habit had suffered. I was determined to take advantage of the snow days to get ten or twenty thousand words in and finish this book.

My image popped on the screen, curls sticking out at odd angles, and it was then I noticed the coffee dribbles on my "Plotting Mysteries & Brewing Coffee" sweatshirt.

My aunt's perfectly styled hair and carefully applied makeup made me feel like a character in desperate need of a rewrite.

Aunt Mary ignored my appearance and smiled. If I'd been talking to my mother, she would have made exactly ten comments about my appearance before saying hello. A comment about my hair. My choice of wardrobe. "Why don't you put on that dress I sent you?" Referring to a body hugging, short, uncomfortable shiny thing she'd sent from

Paris. And "Did you get the make-up kit I sent you? Those moisturizers will do wonders for your skin and fade those freckles." I shook my head, physically trying to shake my mother's comments out. She wasn't here in-person or on Zoom, but she was always in my head.

"It's so nice to see you," Aunt Mary said, her cheerful tone a welcome contrast to the gray day outside.

"You too!" I grinned back at the screen, already feeling the warmth of her virtual presence.

"I'm going stir crazy here!" She threw her hands up in mock despair.

I laughed and took a sip of my coffee, the steam curling upward. "Don't you have Jenny there to keep you company?"

"She's been holed up in her room doing research for the Crimecaster podcast," Aunt Mary said, rolling her eyes with a fond smile.

Just then, Cara walked by the computer. She did a double-take when she saw my face on the screen and doubled back. "Hey, Harper."

"Hey, Cara!" I quickly set my coffee down and instinctively tried to tame my unruly curls with both hands.

"Don't worry, I've got bedhead too," she replied, shoving her messy bun toward the camera. "Your aunt let me stay here because glamping is no fun in a storm, and my house is basically uninhabitable."

Leave it to my aunt to take in anyone who needed a place to stay, just like she did for me. "How can you be bored?" I asked Aunt Mary as Cara wandered back into the kitchen. The sound of cupboard doors opening and closing echoed in the background.

Aunt Mary shook her fists in frustration. "I just miss my projects and being out and about." She paused, glancing toward the kitchen as the faint clank of a teapot reached our ears. She leaned closer to the camera and whispered, "She's making a cup of tea."

"And there's something sinister about that?" I whispered back, unable to keep the grin off my face.

"No," she chuckled, keeping her voice low. "I just don't want her to hear me. You know that large piece of property she owns on the edge of Christmas Tree Forest?"

"Yes," I said, leaning forward in my chair, my curiosity piqued.

"She's selling it to Lila Weston for development."

"What?" I blurted, my voice a little too loud for our whispered conversation.

"I know," Aunt Mary said, her eyes widening. "She told me yesterday. That's how she plans to finance the remodel."

"So she's already decided to stay? She's made the decision before the big reveal?" I asked, lowering my voice again. That was a definite no-no in the Sell It or Stay world, especially for Aunt Mary. The homeowners' reactions and decision process were supposed to be genuine, for the sake of TV drama.

Cara returned, pulling a chair over and plopping down next to Aunt Mary. I decided to channel my inner Jenny Murder and use some of the podcasting skills I'd picked up to ask a few questions. "Can I ask you something?"

"Sure," Cara said, crossing her legs clad in pink yoga pants and taking a careful sip of her tea.

"Why are you selling your property to Lila Weston?"

Cara set her tea down on the dining room table and let out a small laugh. "I should've expected that from you too, Harper. You *are* a mystery writer."

"Me too?" I raised an eyebrow.

"Yes, you too," Cara said, leaning back in her chair. "I'm staying in a house with Jenny Murder. She already grilled me once, and she's been holed up in your old room working on a podcast this whole snowstorm." She leaned forward until the camera captured only her nose and whispered dramatically, "She could at least come out and play Speed Scrabble with your aunt. I've only played like fifty times."

"Do you mind sharing what you told Jenny? The shortened version," I asked, tilting my head and giving Cara a curious look.

Cara shrugged, her shoulders rising and falling with a casualness that didn't quite match the tension in the room. "Sure. I bought that house with money my parents gave me," she said, her tone light but her gaze shifting briefly away from the camera. "My husband ran off with the remodel money right after we signed the Sell It Or Stay contract." Her mouth tightened at the corners, a hint of bitterness leaking through. "I don't want to leave Evergreen Heights or sell. So I'm selling four hundred and ninety acres to Lila to fund the remodel. I'll have a few acres of yard which makes me sad because I don't want to see the land go. But I feel backed into a corner right now and I have no other options. End of story." She chuckled dryly at her own writer's joke, but the humor didn't quite reach her eyes.

Only it wasn't the end of the story, and I could feel the unease settling in my stomach. Jenny was keeping me out of the loop, and I didn't like it one bit. I had helped her countless times, digging up leads and putting the pieces together. For goodness' sake, she was living in my childhood bedroom. And like Goldilocks, she had found everything—my bed, my comforter, my green floral wallpaper—*just right*. It was almost as if she was borrowing my life, and I wasn't sure I appreciated it.

———

When the storm abated, the town opened their doors, only to be greeted by a blank sheet of snow. It was as if someone had shoved a piece of typing paper against everyone's door. The next step in the town's agenda was to clear pathways from parking lots to grocery stores, businesses, the school, and the library.

I took a break from typing a chapter and stood in front of the huge window overlooking the street. I held my mug in both hands, sipping the steaming brew. The streets were no longer quiet. Plows pushed the last bits of snow off while business owners shoveled, trying to find new places to put the snow. I waved at Zoe, who was entering the building.

Bea's two teens paused their shoveling and waved at me. Hopefully, Bea was inside baking up a storm. I paused and laughed at my own joke. I hadn't had any fresh baked goods for two days.

I should get dressed and head downstairs and help Zoe. My phone buzzed as I moved to the closet with Rory in tow to pick out my clothes. I grabbed it off the desk and moved into the walk-in closet.

A text from Zoe:

Still opening at ten?

I texted back:

I'll be down in five minutes and we can discuss.

She texted back:

Running across the street to pick up some goodies from Bea.

I texted back:

Hallelujah!

Rory nosed a winter-white sweater dress with little Christmas trees all over it.

"Good choice, buddy. I feel the Christmas vibes." I grabbed it off the hanger, peeled my flannel pajamas off, and slipped it on. I selected evergreen-colored tights and my white boots. After washing my face and applying some light makeup, I headed down the stairs with Rory in tow.

I took Rory out the back door of the building to pee in the spot Bea's teenage sons had shoveled for me- a snow fort with four ten foot high walls. It was enough space for Rory to do his business. I'm sure he was ready for his long walks again, instead of his ten by ten snowy pee pad.

I wiped his feet and hung my coat up on the back rack before walking down the hall to the cafe. Once in the cafe, the sounds of conversations and laughter on the street made it feel like a holiday. Sure, it was Zoe teasing Bea's teens, but it felt warm and cozy. I felt the urge to drink a Peppermint Latte and put my Christmas Tree back up.

"Boss, I've got the goods, and look who I found at the bakery." Zoe set down the white boxes of baked goods on the counter. Before looking to see who she'd found at the bakery, I opened the box and pulled out a cinnamon roll.

"Oh Bea's baked goods, how I've missed you." I took a ginormous bite, and sticky bits of icing and cinnamon covered my lips like my mother's signature red lipstick. I sighed with relief. "You know," I said, uncharacteristically spewing cinnamon roll from my mouth, "I didn't realize how addicted I am to—"

"Good morning!" Dexter said.

I turned away from him and put my hand over my mouth before hissing to Zoe, "Why didn't you tell me it was him?"

"Where's the fun in that?"

Dexter cleared his throat. "I'm going to interview Lila and Danny. I thought you might want to come."

Come? What? He was inviting me to investigate with him?

"Sure," I mumbled. "Let me grab my coat." I

rushed to the back of the building, stopping at the bathroom to wash my lips and apply fresh lip balm. I scrunched my curls with some water and checked my teeth for cinnamon roll residue. Once I looked presentable, I peeled my coat off the hook and put it on.

"I made you a Double Espresso to go, Boss," Zoe started with a smile, as I re-entered the cafe.

Dexter held up his coffee. "I've got mine." Then held up a paper bag. "With cinnamon rolls to go!" he said with an evident twinkle in his eye.

I didn't know if I could ever eat one of those in front of him again.

As we drove down the winding, snow-packed road, the sun finally broke through the thick gray clouds, casting a golden glow across the snow tunnel created by the drifts on the sides of the road. The silence between us was comfortable, and every time I glimpsed Dexter's profile—his strong jawline, the bit of stubble he hadn't bothered to shave, and the way his dark hair fell just above his eyes—I felt a familiar flutter in my chest. I kept my gaze out the window, hoping the view would distract me.

"Thanks for letting me tag along," I said, fiddling with the buttons on my wool coat. "I was surprised you asked me."

Dexter glanced at me, a small smile curving his lips. "You've proven yourself pretty good at digging up information. Besides," he added, his voice dipping in that way that made my pulse quicken, "it's nice having you around."

My cheeks warmed, and I turned to the window

again to hide the smile tugging at my lips. "You just want me there to soften Lila up for the interview."

"That, too," he admitted with a chuckle. "But I wouldn't mind if we had a little more time together, you know, outside of group campfires and crime scenes."

I raised an eyebrow, the teasing tone coming out before I could help it. "Are you saying I'm more than just a useful sidekick?"

He glanced at me, his eyes meeting mine for a moment that felt like it lasted longer than it should have. "More like a partner in crime-solving," he said, his voice deepening, "and …more than that."

The words hung in the air, making my breath catch. I quickly glanced down at my hands, trying to tamp down the giddy feeling rising in my chest. "So, what's your theory on Lila?" I asked, steering the conversation back on track, though I could still feel the warmth of his words lingering.

"Lila Weston's always had a knack for staying just out of reach when it comes to questions outside of official meetings," he said, the shift in his tone unmistakable. "But her son Danny? He's a wildcard. He definitely does not want his mom's plan to commercialize Christmas Tree Forest to succeed. If there's a loose thread, he might be the one to pull."

I nodded, stealing another sideways glance at him. "Well, let's hope he's feeling chatty today."

Dexter looked at me, and there was a spark in his eyes that I couldn't quite ignore. "With you there, I'm sure he will be. You've got a way of getting people to open up, Harper."

A gentle, heartfelt smile spread across my face. "And what about you, Detective?" I asked softly, my voice coming out quieter than I'd intended. "Am I getting you to open up?"

His hand brushed against mine as he shifted gears, the brief touch sending a little jolt through me. "You've been doing that since the day we met," he murmured.

I turned back to the window, but this time I wasn't looking at the snowy landscape. My heart felt lighter, my pulse still fluttering from his words. Whatever awaited us with Lila and Danny, I couldn't deny that this was about more than just solving a case.

We pulled up in front of Lila's Airbnb. Dexter opened my door and reached out, his hand gently resting on my elbow as I stepped out onto the icy drive. My foot slipped, and before I knew it, he caught me, both arms wrapping firmly around my waist. For a moment, we were inches apart, his warm breath visible in the cold air, and I could feel the steady thrum of his heartbeat against me. I could have stayed there all day, nestled in his embrace, but the front door suddenly swung open, breaking the spell. Danny emerged, dressed in a sharp business suit, his man-bun conspicuously absent.

CHAPTER 11

SECRETS AMONG THE TREES

I BLINKED, momentarily stunned. Gone was the scruffy guy I had expected, the one with a man-bun, a hammock strapped to his back, and that perpetually hungry look. Instead, he stood there in a perfectly tailored navy suit, the sharp lines and soft sheen catching the light with each step. The clean scent of his aftershave reached me—woodsy, with a hint of spice— nothing like the outdoorsy, earthy smells I'd imagined. As he opened the door wider, the quiet rustle of fine fabric replaced the jangle of hiking gear. I could almost taste my surprise, sharp and bitter, like the sting of real- izing I'd been right about him being fake—but there was something deeper, something just out of reach, that I couldn't quite pinpoint yet.

I took a quick sideways glance at Dexter. His face registered shock as well.

Danny stopped in his tracks, a flicker of guilt crossing his face as their eyes met. "Surprised?" he said, forcing a crooked smile that didn't quite reach his eyes. "Guess I clean up better than you thought."

His hand drifted to the back of his neck, a nervous habit, as if he were reaching for a man-bun that wasn't there. His voice dropped, almost sheepishly. "Figured you might not recognize me without the whole starving-camper vibe."

"We have some questions to ask you," Detective Dexter said as he showed his badge.

I'm glad Dexter was doing the talking because I was still picking my chin up off the floor. It gave me time to piece Danny's puzzling behavior into a better picture of who he actually was.

"Who is it, Son?" Lila's voice drifted from an inner room. "Is it the grocery delivery? Or Cara?"

"Neither, Mom. It's the detective and the murder mystery writer/ professor." Danny stuck his suit-clad arm in the direction Lila's voice was coming from. "Go on in."

I expected him to say "Come through" as if we were in some sort of formal British manor.

Lila was perched on the edge of a white wingback chair with a large bank of windows behind her, the sunlight streaming in and casting a soft glow on her honey colored locks. Dressed in an all-white business suit, she looked more like an angel than a corporate mogul. Her smile was warm and inviting, the kind that seemed to welcome you in, but there was a glint in her eye—just a flicker of something sharp, like the edge of a blade hidden behind velvet. As she leaned forward, her voice was smooth and sweet, but there was an unmistakable weight to her words, as though she was used to getting what she wanted—by any means necessary.

She motioned for us to take a seat on one of the two matching white couches flanking her chair. I was feeling like I'd landed in the setting of one of my novels. I was the amateur sleuth out of my depth, challenged by the setting, which was set up to intimidate the visitor.

Once we were seated, Lila picked up a bell and rang it. A uniformed maid appeared, and I did a double take. I didn't know maids existed in Evergreen Heights, or wore uniforms.

"Fredicka, could you bring us some coffee and refreshments?"

Before Fredicka could answer, Lila turned to Detective Dexter, brushing me off as if I were little more than a part of the furniture. "Now, what did you need to ask me?" she said, her tone sweet but her gaze sharp.

I allowed it for now, using the moment to gather my thoughts and quietly observe her. The way she held her head, just slightly tilted, suggested a calculated patience, as if she were carefully playing a part. I focused on every twitch, every flicker in her expression.

"Yes, I need to ask you a few questions about Elmer," Dexter said, his voice low but pressing.

Lila's eyes widened, but just barely. "Oh yes, the poor mentally challenged man who rushed the stage during the town hall meeting."

"Yes," Dexter replied, his gaze steady on her.

She hesitated, then leaned forward and with a whisper of drama said, "I heard he is dead."

Dexter's tone hardened. "Murdered."

Her eyes flickered with something—surprise, or maybe just well-practiced shock. "You don't think I…"

I seized the moment, my voice slicing through the tension. "You did have motive."

Her gaze snapped to me, her face clouding with disdain. "What motive would I have for murdering a demented old man?"

Dexter stepped in, his voice calm but pointed. "Elmer was a retired forestry professor whose opinion and expertise was well-respected in this town."

Lila, perhaps unaware of the shift in her own voice, filled in the rest, her words thick with a hint of bitterness. "And he opposed the project…"

She rose as Fredicka brought a silver tray in with coffee and store-bought cookies. Her hands shook as she set the tray down.

"So no deliveries yet?" Lila said, eyeing the chocolate chip cookies.

"Not yet." Fredicka sat down on the opposite sofa and slumped into the back.

I tensed, waiting for Lila to yell at her.

"How did I do?" Fredicka asked.

"Fine, until you slumped on the couch," she answered with a chuckle.

Lila turned to us. "You'll have to forgive my niece and the theatrics. Playing the maid was her idea. She's trying out for a play at her university."

"Your son is quite the actor too," I stated, watching Lila's eyes narrow ever so slightly. It was as if I'd touched a nerve.

"Let's finish with a few more questions and then

we'd like to speak to Danny," Dexter said, his voice steady as he tried to get the conversation back on track.

"We?" Lila and Fredicka both turned to me, their eyes appraising.

"Yes," Dexter confirmed, a hint of protectiveness in his tone. "Harper has consulted on several cases. She's helping on this one."

Lila's expression hardened, her gaze locking onto mine with a glint of steel. "And you think I'm a suspect?"

I held her stare, letting the silence stretch. "You have a motive," I replied evenly.

She gave a short, humorless laugh, a smirk tugging at one corner of her mouth. "If I murdered everyone who opposed my resorts, I'd be a serial killer with bodies strewn from one side of the country to the other."

"Aunt Lila, don't say that," Fredicka hissed, her face paling as she looked at her aunt.

Lila gave an exaggerated sigh and sat up straighter, crossing her arms with a dramatic flourish. "Fine, I didn't murder him. Is that better?"

Dexter kept his focus, his notebook in hand. "Where did you go after the town hall meeting?"

"I stayed and answered a few questions," Lila said breezily, though I noticed her hand tapping lightly on the table, "before coming here."

She paused, a look of distaste crossing her face as she wrinkled her nose. "Don't forget about that earth woman. I think she still had twigs in her hair from the forest. And she smelled like dirt."

"Fiona?" I asked, my interest piqued. Lila's disdain for Fiona had an edge to it.

"Yes," she replied, rolling her eyes. "That wasn't the first conversation I've had with her. But she's harmless. All talk and no action."

Dexter leaned forward. "Could you clarify?"

"Well, I mean she opposes the development," Lila said, waving a dismissive hand, "but she's not one of those fanatics who carries signs and throws paint at people."

I narrowed my eyes, sensing an edge to her words. "How do you know that?"

Lila raised an eyebrow, as if the answer were obvious. "I had Danny, my right-hand man, look her up, of course."

Because Fredicka wasn't really a maid, she didn't pour us coffee. As Lila pulled out her phone to text Danny and ask him to join us, I took the liberty and served us. I avoided the cookies, knowing back at the cafe I intended to eat another cinnamon roll or two.

Danny entered the room sheepishly, apologizing as he sat down.

"Sorry, I didn't mean to deceive you." Then he glanced at his cousin. "What are you doing in that getup?"

Fredicka giggled, stood and smoothed out her apron. "You aren't the only one who can act."

"So your job is to go into a community and find out who is against the development," I said.

Danny fiddled with his suit buttons before answering. "I thought you'd figured me out at the lecture on Hemlock Trail."

Fredicka threw a pillow at him. "Shagbark hickory. You'd better learn your trees or you're going to get fired from this gig."

Danny threw the pillow back before continuing. "Yes, my job is to feel out the community. This is the first time I've had to dress up as a grungy camper, no offense Detective."

"None taken. But you're going to have to answer a few questions…" Dexter's tone was firm, but before he could go on, I jumped in, the words spilling out before I could stop myself.

"Did Elmer know you were a fake?"

Danny's expression shifted, a flash of surprise crossing his face. "Yes, and Fiona too," he replied, glancing down. "But not in the way you think."

Dexter's brow furrowed. "What do you mean?"

Danny took a deep breath, his shoulders slumping slightly. "They both just thought I was some starving tree-hugger who didn't know anything about the woods. They had no idea Lila Weston is my mom."

I narrowed my eyes, noting the unease flickering in his gaze. "How do you know?"

He shifted in his seat, tugging at his sleeve. "Well, after your lecture, Harper, Fiona, and Elmer all offered to teach me about the forest."

I recalled that moment vividly, the way Elmer had stormed after us, his voice echoing through the parking lot. "You mean after Elmer chased us to the parking lot and he and Fiona fought?"

"They had an argument?" Dexter asked, his pen poised over his notebook.

Danny shook his head, giving a small shrug. "Not

really an argument. Elmer was just going on and on about some bird, and Fiona just said they'd talk about it later."

My eyes narrowed, sensing there was more to it. "And did they?"

"Not while I was with them," Danny replied, scratching his head. "Fiona took us back to her house, and we had some homemade soup and cornbread muffins."

"And then what happened?" I leaned forward, catching every flicker of expression on his face.

"They spent the next hour teaching me tree basics. Fiona's got all kinds of books on trees, and her study is lined with photos of them." He trailed off, his gaze distant, as if the memory had transported him back to Fiona's cluttered, wood-scented study.

We were getting nowhere. If Lila didn't murder Elmer, Danny didn't, and Fiona and Elmer were buddies who helped educate the masses on hemlocks, oaks, maples and shagbark hickories, who and what were left?

"You expected Cara?" I asked.

"Yes, she is coming over." Lila rolled her shoulders back, a defensive posture. Or was she ready to pounce? "To discuss the sale of her property bordering Christmas Tree Forest."

I'd definitely hit a nerve—and uncovered a clue that no one was ready for.

CHAPTER 12
HOME, HEART, AND TIME LIMITS

CARA ARRIVED at Lila Weston's doorstep in sleek black leggings and a deep emerald sweater that set off her complexion. A tailored camel coat, ankle boots, and a patterned scarf completed her polished look with just a hint of flair.

We exited the Airbnb as Cara entered. Dexter paused in the foyer to ask Cara her whereabouts after the town hall meeting.

"I went back to the campsite." She turned and smiled at me. "Hi Harper, staying with your aunt is fun, and she loves word games."

I knew she was referring to the fifty times she said she played Speed Scrabble with her during the snow storm while Jenny was hiding in her room working on the podcast.

As I stepped off the porch, I turned and asked, "Where is Jenny?"

"As far as I know, she's on her way here to talk to Lila."

Inside my head, I clapped my hands together in glee. Had I beat Jenny to interview a suspect? Two could play at this game. If she were going to shut me out and not keep me abreast of her investigation, then I planned to stick with the detective. I leaned on Dexter as he helped me down the icy stairs.

"Watch out for the ice," he said.

I wanted to slip on the ice and have him catch me again, but with my proprioception issues, I'd probably slip, hit my head, get a concussion and end up in the hospital instead. I gingerly stepped over the ice I'd slipped on earlier.

Once seated safely in the SUV, I leaned back and took a deep breath. Dexter started it and waited for it to warm up before blasting the heat. He backed out of the driveway but instead of heading back to the Cozy Corner, he hid in the driveway of a vacant Airbnb which had recently been plowed. They must be expecting guests.

"Let's see where Cara goes after her meeting with Lila."

We didn't have to wait long for a car to exit Lila's drive. A Toyota 4Runner with tinted windows exited the driveway. It passed us, and Dexter put his SUV in gear and followed.

I wasn't sure why I wasn't talking about what we just learned at Lila's house. I was acting as if we were hiding in a room with the three suspects.

Dexter looked determined as the SUV slipped onto the main road.

"Is there a reason we aren't talking?" I whispered.

"Oh," he looked at me as if he just noticed I was in the vehicle. "Sorry, I was thinking about the case."

"So was I," I said, rubbing my hands together more in frustration than for warmth. "We could talk about it."

"What's to talk about?" he said, his eyes on the road.

Keeping thoughts on the case to yourself must be going around. First Jenny. Now Dexter. Not to mention, I hadn't heard from Sage in days. And my aunt had invited a suspect to stay with her during the storm and hadn't told me. The warmth I'd felt between Dexter and me earlier had chilled. I felt iced out.

We followed the Toyota to the Bea's Bakery parking lot. The door opened and Danny hopped out, his man bun and starving camping attire back on. He gave us a wave and walked into the bakery.

"Thanks for taking me along," I opened my door and tested the street for slippage before stepping out.

"I'm sorry," he said as he leaned over the passenger seat. "This case is really frustrating me."

"Me too. Just dead ends." I slammed the door a little too hard. How could our relationship go from hot to cold so quickly? Then I remembered what Cassy had said to me a few days ago about Jake's needs. What did Dexter need? A lead? A suspect with no alibi? I couldn't give him either of those.

I reopened my door. "Come in for a cup of coffee?"

"Sure," he said. "And one of those cinnamon rolls you had earlier."

I knew he was teasing me, but I liked it. And at least we were talking again. Maybe what Dexter needed when he was frustrated was silence. Just like when I was stuck on a plot line, I holed up in my office and turned on some jazz to think.

Dexter and I took our cinnamon rolls and coffees up to the second floor and camped out on the couches. We didn't discuss the case any further. There was nothing to say on that matter.

We talked about my latest novel, teaching, and his current house hunt. He'd been living in Evergreen Heights for almost a year and renting an apartment, which I'd never visited, of course. I used my outside time to teach class, hike with friends, and go on dates with Dexter, usually with other people around.

"Your aunt Mary has shown me three properties. One on the other side of Christmas Tree Forest, but because of its location, it would take me half an hour to drive to work and …"

He paused. I set my cinnamon roll down, careful to wipe my mouth before taking a swig of my Double Espresso. He still hadn't continued.

I set down my mug that had the words "Solving Crimes One Sip at a Time" on it, and said, "You were going to say?"

"Well, it's a half an hour drive. Even if you got a ride to see me. You'd have a limited amount of time you could spend there."

He wanted me to spend time at his house. My stomach felt all warm and gooey like the cinnamon roll sloshing around in there with the Double Espresso.

"Thank you for trying to phrase that so delicately." I crossed my legs and leaned against his shoulder. "I've been upping my outside hours. I've made it to three a few times."

He reached his arm around my back and squeezed my shoulder. "Yes, and I'm proud of you. But no offense, you're like a ticking time bomb when you run out of time. I don't want to put you through that."

I smiled. "You said three houses."

"Yes, the other two are in town and need some work." He sighed heavily.

"Let me guess. Aunt Mary wants you to be the next guest on Sell It Or Stay."

"You've got it. And I don't have time for that. Nor do I want my face plastered all over the television."

Was that panic I saw in his eyes? I'd never seen that look before. Before I had a chance to ask him about it, the calm, cool, serene presence reappeared. He stood and stretched. "I've got to get to work," he said.

I stood and he enveloped me in a bear hug. "I could think of a convenient place for me to live." He released me and nodded to the stairs to my apartment.

My face turned redder than holly berries. "What are you saying?" He knew I didn't believe in shacking up, or whatever people called it these days.

He laughed. "You should see your face. I meant Bea's Bakery. She has an apartment above her shop her son used to live in. On the fourth story. Her family lives on the second and third."

"Yes, Ben, my former bookkeeper's place."

"I'd still be renting for now. But I'd be closer to you." He gave me a peck on the cheek and left before I could say another word.

I gathered our dishes and went down to the bookstore to organize some books that had just come in, thinking about what it would be like to live across the street from Dexter.

———

"Hey Boss, do you have a fever? Your face is all red!" Zoe exclaimed as I placed the dishes in a bin behind the counter.

"No, I'm fine. Where are the boxes of new children's books?"

"I opened them and put them in the stock room. Some of them got a little wet. We may have to ship them back."

I went into the stock room and grabbed a stack of Jan Brett books and rejoined Zoe at the cafe counter. "I'm going to put these dry ones on the shelf."

"Keep a count," she advised. "Rosy hasn't put them in the system yet."

"Will do," I answered.

The bell above the door chimed, drawing my attention from the stack of books I was counting. Fiona stepped into the Cozy Corner, bringing the scent of pine and wood smoke with her. Her cheeks were flushed from the cold, and her silver-peppered chestnut braid hung loosely over one shoulder. She wore a patched wool coat over her flannel shirt, with sturdy hiking boots that left a trail of melting snow on the floor.

"Harper," she greeted in that calm, steady voice of hers. "I heard you've been asking questions about what happened after the town hall meeting."

I felt a flicker of surprise, but quickly masked it. "You and everyone else in town," I replied, setting the books down and crossing my arms. "I didn't think you were that interested in town gossip."

Fiona took a step closer, her boots thudding softly on the wooden floor. "I'm not," she said simply. "But I cared about Elmer. He didn't deserve what happened to him." Her eyes, the color of moss-covered bark, flicked to the map of town on the wall, with Christmas Tree Forest highlighted in evergreen.

"But I was there," she said quietly. "I saw Danny lead Elmer off the stage. It seemed...odd." Her gaze shifted to the map on the wall.

There was something in her tone, a hint of unease. "Odd how?" I asked, trying to sound casual but feeling a tightening in my chest.

She shrugged slightly, though I noticed her fingers tightening around the strap of her hand-woven basket. "Danny was quick to get him offstage, almost like he was trying to hurry him away before anyone else could ask questions. And with Lila discussing the desecration of the forest, all eyes were on her. Not Danny and Elmer."

"And Elmer ended up at the hospital." I said, my voice quieter now. "But he left before anyone could keep him there."

"Exactly." Fiona's eyes met mine, calm but piercing. "Danny could've followed Aunt Mary to the hospital, used the commotion as a distraction." She let the words hang in the air. "Who's to say he didn't go after Elmer when he slipped out?"

Before I could respond, the door swung open again, bringing a gust of cold air and Danny himself. He strode in with a practiced ease, dressed in his version of outdoorsy-chic: expensive camping clothes that looked freshly bought, not trail-worn. His jacket alone probably cost more than my entire winter wardrobe, and his man-bun was perfectly styled, as usual.

How had I not noticed the expensive clothing before? I'm pretty sure he'd rubbed his previous outfits and face with mud to make himself fit the homeless camper character.

For the briefest moment, a shadow passed over Fiona's expression. "Danny's the type who wouldn't know an oak from a maple if you pointed it out to him," she whispered as Danny walked to the cafe counter, a hint of scorn in her voice. "But that doesn't mean he didn't kill Elmer."

"Am I interrupting something?" he asked, a slight smirk on his lips. There was a trace of amusement in his tone, as if the idea of me and Fiona talking was funny to him.

Fiona turned to face him, her expression hardening just slightly. "No, Danny. We were just finishing up." She glanced back at me. "See you around, Harper." Without another word, she headed for the door, her boots crunching on the salt the patrons had brought in from outside.

I watched her leave, that knot in my chest tightening. Fiona's words echoed in my head as I thought about Danny leading Elmer away, Aunt Mary taking him to the hospital, the timing of it all. And as Danny lingered by the door, that faint smirk still on his lips, I couldn't shake the feeling that he knew more than he was letting on. Maybe Fiona was right—maybe he'd used the chaos to cover his tracks.

CHAPTER 13
SHADOWS OF DOUBT

I CALLED Dexter right away and let him know what Fiona had said about Danny.

He promised to follow up but I could tell he didn't think Danny was the murderer.

I finished shelving the books, counting the water damaged ones, and filled out a report online on the office computer. Rosy could handle the rest when she came in the next day.

When I entered the cafe, Jenny was sitting at the counter, sipping what I'm sure was a Peppermint Latte. It was her favorite winter coffee drink.

"I have a bone to pick..." I didn't finish my sentence because when she turned to look at me, her eyes were red and puffy, like she'd been crying for three days.

"Way to be sensitive, Harper," Zoe said. This was serious. Zoe wasn't calling me "boss" or joking around.

"What's going on? Cara said you've been holed up in your room working on the podcast for the entire snow storm."

"Podcast? What?" She shook her head and blew her nose loudly into a tissue Zoe handed her. "It's my brother. He ran away from the program Dexter got him into at The Mountain Challenge Academy."

"Oh," I said. I couldn't think of anything else to say.

She sniffled. "I've been using all my contacts to find him."

Zoe handed her a snickerdoodle. Because cookies fix everything. She took the cookie and set it down absent-mindedly. "They won't take him back, you know. I should have listened to him. He said he hated camping and the woods."

"What does he like?" I asked, trying to get her to think about something else.

"He likes art, of all things. Before he got in trouble with gangs, he used to spend hours at The Metropolitan Museum of Art." She chuckled at the memory. "He got kicked out of museums after he tatted up and started wearing gang colors."

An idea was brewing inside my head. I couldn't say it out loud yet, not until I talked to a few people. "Does he have his phone?" I asked.

"Probably. I can't imagine him leaving camp without taking it out of the lockbox the director stored the electronics in." She took a sip of her latte. "But he won't answer me. I've tried texting and calling him."

"I'll be back in fifteen minutes." I said, jogging toward the stairs. "Don't go anywhere."

"Boss, don't you have an appointment with Edgar?"

I slid to a stop. Rory ran into me and we fell in a heap.

"Yes, Edgar. He can help too," I said to myself as I

stood up and brushed down my dress. "It's on Zoom today in half an hour. He doesn't want to drive in this stuff." I waved an arm in the direction of the windows displaying the snow banked on the street.

Although Jenny was still distraught, I didn't dare soothe her by laying out my entire plan before I had even an inkling of proof everyone was on board. I simply promised her I would help and told her she wasn't alone. We spent the next half an hour with me sharing stories from my many faux pas during my summer in Paris. After a few stories, she loosened up and the tension released as she rolled on the floor laughing at me.

When it was time for my appointment, I clicked open the Zoom meeting with Edgar. Jenny hung out in my living room while she waited for me to get the last piece of my plan in place. Rory opted to hang with her, probably because she had food and I did not.

As Edgar's face popped on the screen, he straightened his laptop. He opened his mouth, to say "Hello" I'm sure, but I interrupted him with my plan.

When I finished laying out my plan, "so you see, if you look over his profile and don't find anything like serial killer genes or anything, then maybe my parents would take him on as an intern," Edgar ran his fingers through his silver afro and then drummed his fingers on his desk. He looked as if he needed a moment to catch up.

"Slow down, Harper. I'd have to meet him first. In person."

"Oh," I slid my chair back and thought for a minute.

Before I could say another word, he explained, "Think about how you would sound on paper."

"Oh yeah. Autistic Agoraphobic seeks intern position. Not to mention my wardrobe choices." I tapped the desk with a pencil.

"Ex-gang member seeks internship," I continued. "I see what you're saying. But you'd meet him?"

"Yes, I'd be happy to help Jenny in any way I can."

I jumped up, ran to the glass doors of my office/bedroom and yelled down to Jenny. "It's a 'yes' from him!"

Then I went back in and settled in for my session with Edgar.

Jenny texted her brother Brian, explaining that she knew why he ran away and that she might have an opportunity for him involving his love of art if he would just text her back.

We watched together as the three dots danced across the screen and finally:

No more camping?

Jenny texted back:

None. I promise.

She continued the text conversation in private while I ordered sandwiches from The Sandwich Shop, hoping Robin would deliver them.

I put down my phone and studied the murder board for a second. I hadn't told Jenny, or any of the students who'd been helping on the case, about Fiona's visit and the new evidence against Danny. I wondered if Jenny knew Danny wasn't the starving tree-hugging camper he claimed to be. I moved Danny to the number one suspect position.

Jenny finished her phone conversation with her brother and joined me by tackling me in a hug so forceful it sent me to the ground.

"Thank you so much. I was so worried about him."

Rory thought we were on the floor to play with him, so he joined us, biting my hair and my dress.

"Stop it Rory. You're welcome," I said as I pulled my hair out of Rory's teeth and rolled away from him.

As I stood, Rory turned his attention to Jenny, licking the crumbs of a Snickerdoodle off her cheeks. She got her feet and hands under her and rose to downward-facing dog. She paused to study the murder board upside down.

"Danny?" she asked.

"Yes, I'll tell you all about it after you give me the details about your brother."

She walked her feet to her hands and stood. "He'll be here tonight. You'll get to meet him. I got him a bus ticket and talked to The Mountain Challenge Academy. He's in the clear for now."

Now if my dad would keep his word, the attorney, Victoria, would do her job, Edgar would meet him and give him a glowing behavioral analysis, then…

"Now tell me about Danny."

"After I take Rory out."

"I'll do that," she said. "And wait for our sandwiches."

Robin did not deliver the sandwiches. All of my students were finally back in class after two snow days.

Jenny and I ate our wraps, and I filled her in on the visit to Lila's home, Danny's appearance and job, and Fiona's visit to the Cozy Corner. After she was caught up, she said, "Feel like a trip to Christmas Tree Forest tomorrow?"

"Do you think they'll have the campground cleared?"

"Does it matter?"

————

The next day, Jenny and I planned our visit to Christmas Tree Forest for after story hour and The Classics, who finally made it back to the cafe and stayed extra long after being cooped up for days. They talked about Elmer, his awards, Christmas Tree Forest, and a little bit of politics. Elmer's funeral had been postponed due to the weather, but it looked like, weather-permitting, it would be tomorrow. Sometimes these winter storms got a second wind and just when you thought it was over, it wasn't.

Jenny had her Jeep Renegade warmed and ready to go when The Classics began to thin out.

"Come on, my car's out front, warmed and ready to leave." She stopped and waved at Dr. Dennis, who was putting on his wool coat. "I thought they'd never leave."

"Okay, wait, just one more thing." I turned to Edgar, who was still chatting with another Classic. "Excuse me, Edgar, you said Elmer won awards?"

"Oh yes, for his research in forestry, his papers, and discoveries on species that were thought to be extinct. We used to joke at the university that every quarter he'd have a new award." He shook his head and chuckled at the memory. "And now he's gone."

Jenny grabbed my arm, pulling me away from the conversation and toward the door. I waved and mouthed, "I'm sorry."

"Let's go," she hissed.

"That was important," I said. "Don't be rude."

———

I crouched low behind the massive oak, pressing my back against the rough bark. The cold bit through my gloves, but I barely noticed. Beside me, Jenny was fiddling with her phone, setting it to record, her breath visible in the chilly air. We hadn't meant for things to escalate this way. We just wanted to ask Danny a few questions for the *Crimecaster* podcast. But now, hidden behind this tree, we were witnessing something much bigger than a simple interview.

Through a gap in the branches, I could see Anora trekking through the snow, clutching a folder like it was her last lifeline. Her cheeks were flushed red from the cold, but her eyes were hard with determination. Whatever was inside the folder, it was important. It had to be, judging by the way she held onto it.

The crunch of footsteps nearby made me freeze, my breath catching in my throat. I glanced at Jenny, who gave me a quick nod, her eyes wide with excitement. We both leaned forward to get a better look as Danny came stumbling out of the trees. His face was flushed too, but not just from the cold. I could see the frustration etched into every line of his body, his fists clenching and unclenching at his sides.

"Anora, what are you doing out here?" His voice broke the stillness, rough and trembling with anger. Even from where I was hiding, I could hear the desperation in it.

"I could ask you the same thing." Anora's voice was steady, but I could see the way her knuckles tightened around the folder. "I know about Elmer's research on the Cerulean Warblers, Danny. He found evidence they nest right in the middle of your mom's development plans. If this information gets out, the whole project is done for."

My pulse quickened. Cerulean Warblers. I knew they were rare, even protected. If they really were nesting here, there was no way the development could go forward. I shot a look at Jenny, who was mouthing "goldmine," her phone trained on the unfolding scene.

Danny's face darkened. "That's exactly why it can't get out," he spat, his voice cracking. "You don't get it, Anora. My mom—she's counting on this. If this project falls apart, she'll lose everything."

The tension in the air was thick enough to choke on. I could see Danny take a step closer, his eyes pleading now, desperation clinging to his every word. "It's not just about the money. It's about starting over, giving us a chance after everything that happened with Dad. Don't ruin that."

I felt my heart twist as I watched Anora. For a moment, it seemed like she was considering what he said, but then her expression hardened. "And you think that justifies destroying the forest?" Her voice cut through the cold air like a knife. "Elmer was trying to protect these birds. He saw the bigger picture. You don't."

Before I could even process what was happening, Danny lunged forward, grabbing Anora's arm. "Give me the research!" he shouted, his voice echoing through the quiet forest. My breath hitched, and Jenny's phone wavered in her hand.

I felt like I was watching it all happen in slow motion—Anora struggling to wrench free, Danny shoving her, the way her feet slipped out from under her. Then there was the sudden drop, the sickening thud as her head hit a hidden rock beneath the snow.

"Anora!" Danny's scream ripped through the air as he scrambled down the bank toward her. My stomach dropped when I saw the crimson bloom spreading across the snow beside her head. I reached for Jenny's arm, my fingers digging into her sleeve.

Jenny kept recording, her face pale but determined. The weight of what had just happened settled over us like a fog. My heart pounded in my ears as I squeezed Jenny's arm tighter, the same thought racing through my mind over and over—we had just witnessed a tragedy unfold before our eyes, and every second of it was caught on tape.

CHAPTER 14
STRANGER IN THE HOSPITAL

DETECTIVE DEXTER LED DANNY AWAY in handcuffs. Paramedics carefully lifted Anora's limp body onto a stretcher and loaded her into the ambulance.

Jenny checked the recording to make sure she'd caught it all before adding, "Well, that's a wrap," as she stuck her phone back in her coat pocket.

"I hope Anora's going to be okay." I examined the snowbank she'd fallen into. "What do you mean, that's a wrap?"

"Come on, I want to edit the podcast and get out a special edition. This is juicy stuff. Elmer has research about some bird that will halt the development. Danny knocks him off and then goes for Anora."

"Where's the folder?" I asked.

"What?"

"She was clutching a green folder when she fell. It's what Danny was trying to grab from her." I kneeled down and dug in the snow until Sage, who arrived with camera in hand, stopped me.

"You can't dig here, it's a crime scene. Detective Dexter asked me to take photos."

"It's not really a crime scene, is it?" I asked as I stood and continued to poke at the snow with the toe of my boot, like Rory did with her snout when I told her to stop digging.

Sage snapped a lens on and the shutter clicked as she captured photos of Anora's blood on the rock and snow.

"What do you mean, it's not a crime scene?" Sage paused and tilted her head like a bird.

"Listen, Jenny has the whole argument and accident, and I repeat *the accident,* recorded on her phone." I pointed at Jenny, who was at the top of the hill motioning for me to join her.

Sage scoffed, folding her arms. "Let me guess—she wants to go edit and release a special bonus podcast episode."

I shot her a pleading look. "Yes, and she's going to announce we caught the killer."

Sage took a step closer, eyes narrowing. "Didn't we, though?"

Before I could respond, Jenny's voice cut through the tension, sharp and insistent, from the top of the hill. "Come on, Harper! Don't give Sage the scoop!"

I clenched my jaw, glancing up at Jenny, who stood with her hands on her hips, watching us like she was ready to run down the snowbank.

"She's not giving me the scoop and you can't release that podcast episode." Sage let the strap catch the camera when she dropped it. In five quick steps, she crested the hill and stood nose to nose with Jenny. "I see you haven't regained your journalistic integrity, if you ever had any."

Jenny huffed and took a step back.

"Hand me the phone," Sage said, towering over her. She whipped off her scarf and threw it to the ground. Her blonde pixie-cut stood on end and the way the shadows hit her face, she looked like a troll.

"I'm not giving you my phone." Jenny took a step back and tripped over a log, landing butt-first in the snow.

They continued to argue. I ignored them and took the opportunity to dig around in the snow. "The folder is not here."

"Play the recording," Sage said, her face the color of a red maple leaf in the fall.

"Guys!" I yelled while running up the hill. I slid to a stop in between them. "Did you hear what I said? The folder with Elmer's research is gone."

Sage paused and looked down the hill at the crime scene I'd just contaminated and dug up.

"You!" She froze. "There are some boot prints down there that don't belong to us or the Paramedics."

"That's what I've been trying to tell you. Someone took Elmer's research. And it wasn't Danny. He's in a jail cell by now."

Sage slipped back down the hill and took some photos of the boot prints leading into the woods.

"Let's follow them," Jenny suggested.

"Yes, let's do," Sage said.

I glanced at my watch. I still had a good hour left. I

set a timer for forty-five minutes, just to make sure I had time to get back home.

We followed the boot prints through the woods for a good ten minutes before we hit a trail that led to the campground. The boot prints continued to the parking lot where a snowplow whizzed past us and cleared every trace of any print away.

"Well, that's a dead end," Jenny said.

Sage leaned forward, her eyes intense. "No, I can use the print to find out what kind of boot, and then we—"

Jenny snorted, crossing her arms with a smirk. "Do a boot check of everyone in the tri-state area?"

I shot her a look, feeling the familiar heat of frustration rise. "No—just the suspects," I replied, keeping my voice steady but firm. Jenny's laugh grated, but I kept my focus on Sage, who looked like she was already working out the details in her head.

"You can't say anything about the missing folder or the boot prints on the podcast," Sage warned. "You'll tip the killer's hand. They'll dump the boots and burn the evidence."

Jenny stomped her boot on the freshly plowed parking lot. "Now I don't have anything to say."

"Yes, you do." I patted her on the back. "Say what you were going to say."

"Danny Weston is the killer. The case is wrapped up." I smiled.

"And if he is innocent?" Sage said.

I walked to Jenny's car. With my hand on the handle, I said, "You and Dexter can prove that."

"I don't understand," Sage said.

"Me either. I mean, sure, I want to release this juicy stuff." Jenny patted her pocket.

"Here's the thing. If you say the case is over. The killer is behind bars. The real killer will let down his or her guard. They'll keep wearing the boots." I hopped in the passenger seat while Sage and Jenny continued to process. I opened the door a crack. "Come on, let's go Jenny."

"Brilliant," she said as she slipped in the driver's seat and pushed the start button.

I rolled down my window and said to Sage, "I'll tell Zoe to keep an eye out for the boots. So send me the info on them once you have it."

Sage nodded, her eyes darting to the shadows as if she sensed unseen eyes on us. She didn't say a word, just cast a final glance in my direction before turning away. Her footsteps crunched softly over the snow as she made her way back to the woods, where Anora's bloodstain lay like a dark secret on the white ground, waiting to be captured in her lens.

———

Jenny released her bonus episode, reporting Danny's attack on Anora, who was in the hospital in a coma. She also named him as Elmer's killer.

I texted the college students, who were now officially calling themselves The Murder Club, and let them know the case still had some loose ends. I sent out a group text:

Meet at my place at 7pm.

I invited Dexter too, but he declined. He was busy questioning Danny and wrapping up the case. His words, not mine.

At 6:55 p.m., Jenny texted me and said:

> Be there a few minutes late. I'm forwarding you an anonymous tip.

She sent me a photo of a typed note:

"Jenny, you need to know that Elmer wasn't just researching the Cerulean Warbler. His files contain more than bird sightings—they include documents on some questionable activities involving certain people in town. I'm talking about unethical practices that could ruin careers if they came to light. Cara's husband was one of them, and it's no coincidence that he vanished when he did. Dig deeper into Elmer's research, and you'll find more than just birdwatching notes. There's a reason someone wanted that folder kept hidden."

I texted back:

> Wow!

Before everyone arrived, I studied the murder board and moved Danny out of the number one suspect space. I picked up Cara's photo and moved it to the top of the board.

Ryan, Ethan, Robin, Jake, and Cassy came in together, all talking at the same time. Rory joined the conversation by howling.

I shushed him and threw him a chew toy.

Jake set his backpack down on the kitchen counter. "What are we doing here? Jenny said the case was closed."

"Yes, we all listened to the podcast…" Cassy started.

I faced the students and explained Jenny's tactic. "What Jenny did on the podcast was a strategic misdirect," I said. "By releasing some false information about the case, she aimed to provoke a reaction from the real killer. The idea is to relieve the pressure and to make them slip up or take some kind of action that could reveal their identity. It's risky, but sometimes, it's the only way to shake loose the truth."

"What kind of action?" Ethan said, as he set down a bakery bag.

"Wear boots," I replied matter-of-factly.

"I don't understand," Robin said with a quizzical look.

"Let me make some coffee and after Jenny arrives, I'll let her share some new information. Jake, we're going to need your computer hacking skills."

I scooped the coffee into a filter while Robin took mugs out of the cabinet and arranged them on the counter.

"I'll take that bag of baked goods," Cassy said. Ethan handed her the bag and she opened it. "Yum. Cranberry and white chocolate cookies."

"And I grabbed some ginger snaps," he added. "They're on the bottom."

Robin turned and sniffed the air. "I can smell the ginger. Those are my favorite."

"I know," Ethan said, his face coloring the shade of the cranberries in the cookies.

I guess young and thirty-something Emily Dickinson-type recluse love was in the air.

Jenny breezed in with another bag of sweets. "Oh," she said as she plopped them on the counter. "Someone beat me to the sweets."

"That would be Ethan," Robin said as she grabbed a ginger snap off the tray and popped it in her mouth. "These are my favorite."

Jenny's eyes widened as she studied Ethan. He ignored her and stared at Robin with a lopsided, goofy grin.

The coffee maker buzzed, signaling the end of the brew cycle. I clapped my hands together. "Enough chatting. Grab a coffee and a snack and let's gather round the murder board."

With seats from the dining room table, we formed a semicircle in front of the board. I stood and filled everyone in on the information Sage had sent me about the boots.

"Like I said, the podcast episode Jenny released was to get the real killer to relax and get sloppy. Whoever stole the folder Elmer gave Anora from the crime scene left boot prints in the snow. Sage has identified what type of boot it is. So we are looking for Trekker boots size nine women or seven men."

Ryan sounded doubtful. "That's small for a man."

"What color?" Ethan asked, his curiosity evident.

Robin let out a small sigh. "We can't tell color from a boot print, Ethan."

"Oh." His face went pink as he realized his mistake. I hid a smile, watching him shift uncomfortably under Robin's blunt response.

"Not exactly true," Jake offered. "For that type of boot, there are three colors offered. Pink. Green. Espresso." He held up his phone with the L.L.Bean website app as proof.

Jenny stood. "There's more. As you can see, Harper put Cara on the top of the murder board."

"What does she have to do with it?" Cassy asked.

"She's trying to sell her property bordering Christmas Tree Forest to Lila Weston for development." I explained.

"Yes, her husband took their remodel money and ran with it. Cara has to choose the sell option if she doesn't come up with the money for the remodel." Jenny added as she tapped the map of Christmas Tree Forest and Cara's adjoining five hundred acres.

"There's more." I paused and pointed to Jake. "This is where you come in. Jenny got an anonymous note saying, and I quote, 'unethical practices that could ruin careers if they came to light. Cara's husband was one of them, and it's no coincidence that he vanished when he did.'"

"Can you email that note to me, Jenny?" Jake asked. He stood and moved to the dining room table, dragging his chair along with him.

"I can email you a picture of it. It's a typed note."

"Like on a typewriter?" Jake asked, his eyebrows raised.

Jenny pulled the note out of her pocket and held it out to me. "Yes, like on a typewriter."

He backtracked from the table, muttering something to himself as he grabbed the paper. "I may be able to tell what kind of typewriter this was typed on as well. Will that help?"

"Yes," I replied, already feeling a flicker of hope.

Robin leaned forward, eager. "What can we do?"

Cassy jumped up, brushing crumbs off her hands. "I'll get Jake another coffee and a plate of cookies so he can focus," she said with a wink.

I turned to the others. "Ethan, Ryan, Robin—go do some interviews, if you don't mind."

"Mind?" Ryan's eyes lit up, a grin spreading across his face. "This is super cool."

"Cara is staying with my aunt until she can move back to the campground. Can you go over and ask her a few questions about her land? The offer from Lila? And if you feel brave enough, ask about her husband."

Robin typed notes on her phone as I spoke. "Got it."

"I'll let my aunt know you're coming." I picked up my phone and shot her a text.

Jenny grabbed her backpack. "I'm going to interview Lila Weston."

"Do you think that's wise?" I asked.

Jenny slid her leather jacket on. "I talked to her on the phone. That's why I was late. She asked me to come. She wants to share her side of the story."

"Don't go alone. Take Ethan or Ryan with you."

She sized them both up and pointed at Ryan, the bulkier, more muscular co-ed, but the romantic in me thought it was to give Robin and Ethan more time together.

After everyone left for their assignments, Cassy and I joined Jake at the dining room table. After five minutes of silence, except for the clicking of Jake's keyboard, I stood and stretched.

"I'm going to take Rory for a quick walk."

"Want me to come?" Cassy asked.

"No. It's fine."

At the word walk, Rory sprung from his place in front of the fireplace and pranced to the door. I followed, grabbed my coat, slipped my boots on, and snatched the leash. I opened the door, and he zoomed down the stairs, almost knocking down Dexter in his haste, who was coming up the stairs.

"Oh, Rory!" I scolded.

Dexter righted himself and held onto the railing for a moment. "I thought I was a goner," he said.

Ever since I'd increased my outside time, Rory had gotten more rambunctious and out of control. Maybe it was time for obedience school. This isn't the first time I'd thought that, like me, Rory lacked social skills.

"Walk with me?" I asked.

"Sure, I wanted to catch you up on the case," he said as we descended the stairs.

Once outside in the crisp night, the stars sparkling above us, I wished for a moment that we were walking out of our building together. Not because of a case, but because we were married. I looked down to hide my flushed face.

Dexter didn't notice. Rory dragged me to the end of the block before Dexter took the leash and reined him in.

"The case?" I leaned forward, curiosity sparking.

Dexter's eyes glinted. "Oh, you're never going to guess who turned up at the hospital."

"Who?" My mind raced through possibilities.

He leaned in, lowering his voice. "Cara's husband."

My eyebrows shot up. "And she didn't know?"

Dexter shook his head, a faint smirk playing at the corner of his mouth. "And *he* didn't know either."

I frowned, searching his expression. "What do you mean, *he* didn't know?"

"He has amnesia," Dexter explained, voice hushed with intrigue. "Apparently, he was in some sort of accident. Details are still foggy."

"And how did no one notice? Not a single staff member recognized him?" My mind spun, piecing together the implications.

Dexter shrugged, glancing around as if the snow-covered evergreens might be listening. "He's not from around here. After marrying Cara, he worked out of town... until he disappeared."

I exhaled slowly, the truth settling in like a dark cloud. "With her money."

Dexter's gaze met mine, serious now. "And now, he's back—but without a clue about who he is... or what he did."

CHAPTER 15
PIECES OF THE PUZZLE

"I DON'T THINK Danny killed Elmer," I said, changing the course of the conversation.

"We have him on Anora's attempted murder. She's the State DNR representative overseeing the Christmas Tree Forest Commercial Development. I think the case is sealed up tight." Rory ran circles around the gazebo at the center of the park while we talked.

"And yet you just spoke of Cara's husband as if he could have something to do with it."

Dexter shoved both hands in his pockets and pushed his shoulders back, a sign he didn't want to hear any more theories. "How could Cara's husband have killed Elmer? As far as we know, he was in the hospital or lying on the side of the road somewhere."

I nodded, determined. "Let's find out. I'll go to the hospital with you."

Dexter frowned, crossing his arms. "Why would he want to see you?"

I raised an eyebrow. "What do patients do in the hospital?"

"Watch TV and wander around in gowns with their backsides exposed," he deadpanned.

Suppressing a smirk, I shot back, "Read books. I'll have some sent over in the morning, and we can visit in the afternoon."

Just then, Rory finished his laps, pawing at the ground and barking in excitement.

Dexter glanced down, smiling. "I think he's ready to go."

Once back outside the Cozy Corner, Rory and I lingered for a moment as Dexter and I made plans for him to pick me up the next day. After agreeing on a time, he gave me a quick peck on the cheek before heading to his car. As he opened the door, a pang of guilt hit me. I knew Jenny was planning to talk about the note she received on her next podcast, but knowing her, she likely hadn't shared it with the police.

Did I share it? Or let her take responsibility for keeping it under wraps until her big reveal? I let Rory in the door, skidded to Dexter, and grabbed his coat sleeve. He turned and leaned down. Our noses touched, and he pulled me closer, our lips meeting softly at first, then deepening as his hand slid gently to the back of my neck, holding me there as if he'd been waiting for this moment forever.

When he released me, I stumbled backward, my heart racing and my mind spinning. The world seemed to blur for a moment, as though nothing else mattered but the lingering warmth of his kiss.

He reached his hand out to steady me. His smile

was a mix of pride and concern, his eyes searching mine as he steadied me, like he wasn't sure if he'd swept me off my feet or knocked me off balance.

"You okay?" he asked, his voice low and warm, the hint of amusement in his tone doing little to hide the nervous edge in his eyes. It was as if he was trying to gauge if the kiss had been too much, too soon, or exactly what we both had wanted.

"Yes," I answered, but it sounded more like a deflating balloon, hissing and squeaky, than a sexy, breathless response. Awkward. Par for my romantic relationships. What was I talking about? A kiss far superseded any of my wildest dreams and topped any romance, imagined or real in my life.

I forgot to tell him about the note. I stumbled to the door of the Cozy Corner, let myself in, leaned up against the wall next to the kid's coat rack, and slid down on the floor, both my mittened hands on my face. I stayed that way until Rory pulled at a mitten. I'd never been kissed like that before. That kiss superseded all thoughts of the case.

I took Rory back up to the apartment and made a beeline for the bathroom. I splashed cold water on my face. I looked at my reflection. A warm flush bloomed across my cheeks, making my freckles stand out like tiny constellations. How could I rejoin Cassy and Jake? They'd notice, wouldn't they? My phone buzzed. I pulled it out of my coat pocket and dropped it in the sink. I plucked it out and wiped the screen with a hand towel. It was a text from Dexter. I hoped it was a declaration of his love or how much he enjoyed the kiss, or maybe even a marriage proposal. I opened it:

See you at 3pm tomorrow. Don't forget
to send the books in the morning.

My red flush turned from feelings of love to feelings of frustration with one text. I'm glad I didn't share the note with him.

I texted back:

Okay

I let my coat slip off my shoulders and fall on the floor. I picked it up and grabbed my phone. I stepped out of the bathroom and headed straight to the kitchen, brewing another cup of coffee I didn't need. But at least it kept my hands busy while I wrestled with the rush of first-kiss bliss tangled up in the frustration of unreadable texts and men who couldn't express a single feeling.

As the coffee brewed, I remembered the new info about Cara's husband. Something seemed really fishy about the fact that he was a John Doe in our local hospital. Something didn't add up. It would make sense if he were a patient with amnesia in another state, like some of my favorite romcoms: Famous author wrecks car in snowbank three states away from her home. Handsome doctor takes her in and she stays at his guest house and writes a bestseller before she remembers who she is.

But a local? Evergreen Heights scrutinized every newcomer. Hadn't Robin noticed Professor Demetriz last month because he was an out-of-towner in The Sandwich Shop? Let's face it. Evergreen Heights is nosy.

"More coffee, anyone?" I asked, as the brew cycle finished.

Jake raised his mug without saying a word. Cassy grabbed it and joined me in the kitchen.

Cassy refilled his mug as she said, "You're not going to believe what Jake found."

I poured myself a cup and grabbed a ginger snap. "You two aren't going to believe what I found out tonight, either."

Cassy opened the fridge and pulled out the heavy whipping cream and handed it to me. I poured a bit into a milk frothing cup and picked up the frothing wand. Cassy set down Jake's mug and poured herself a mug. I frothed the heavy whipping cream and poured some on top of each of our mugs.

We carried our coffees to the dining room table, and I couldn't hold back any longer. I leaned forward, voice low but urgent. "You're not going to believe who's still in town—and in the hospital."

"Cara's husband," Jake said, cutting me off before I could spill the news.

I blinked, taken aback. "What? How did you…?"

A smug grin tugged at his lips. "I hacked into the hospital's security system. I wanted to keep an eye on Anora, just in case someone tried to finish the job."

"He was just snooping," Cassy said, rolling her eyes as she leaned back in her chair. She folded her arms, then added, "But something didn't sit right about that note Jenny got. If Cara's husband was tangled up in the corruption in Evergreen Heights, why would he take her money and vanish?"

I raised my eyebrows, feeling the weight of the revelation. "He didn't get far—he's at the hospital with amnesia," I said, though I was sure they'd figured that part out.

"And guess who's been visiting him?" Jake spun his laptop around so the screen faced me, the grainy hospital footage frozen mid-frame.

I leaned in, narrowing my eyes. "Cara!" I watched her stand at the nurse's station, as unmistakable as ever. "Yep, that's her." I took a step back, frowning. "How could Dexter miss this?"

"That's the thing," Jake said, his fingers tapping the laptop's edge. "This footage was wiped from the hospital's system. I had to dig to get it, so officially, there's no evidence she was ever there."

"But surely the nurses remember her face, right? I mean, they'd know who she is."

Jake hesitated, shrugging. "I just find the digital footprints. You're the theory expert."

"Wait." Cassy held up a hand, her brows knitting together. "Two questions. How many times did she visit? And was the same nurse on duty each time?"

Jake's fingers flew across the keyboard, his gaze narrowing in focus. "She came twice," he said, adjusting his glasses as he studied the screen. "And...it doesn't add up."

Cassy and I exchanged a glance, then spoke at once. "What?"

"It's strange," he muttered, his face lit by the glow of the screen. "Both visits were around midnight—after visiting hours. And yeah, the same nurse was on duty both times."

Cassy leaned forward. "Can you pull up the nurse's image?"

With a few clicks, Jake zoomed in, revealing the tired face of a woman in her thirties, wearing lilac scrubs. "Printing it now," he said.

The printer whirred to life, spitting out the photo, and without another word, the three of us bolted from the dining room, coffees abandoned. We took the stairs two at a time, adrenaline propelling us up to my office, where the printer hummed in the corner. Jake reached the door first, but Cassy and I weren't far behind.

The photo sat fresh on the tray, still warm. We all leaned in, eyes fixed on the image of the nurse with those tired, hollow eyes in her lilac scrubs, staring back at us.

"Now, why would she be meeting Cara after hours?" Cassy murmured, breaking the silence, but none of us had an answer.

This was only the beginning of something much darker.

As we studied the photo, the quiet of my office broke with the sudden creak of the apartment door below. Footsteps followed, then Robin's voice drifted up, sounding eager. "Where are you guys?"

"We're up in my office!" I called back, leaning over the railing.

"You're not going to believe what Ethan and I found out," she announced, her tone promising secrets.

I glanced back at Cassy and Jake, unable to contain my grin. "Hold tight, Robin! You're not going to believe what *we* found out."

With the nurse's photo in my hand, we barreled

down the stairs, nearly tripping over each other in our hurry, a herd of excited investigators.

Robin and Ethan stood by the murder board, Robin's arms crossed and Ethan looking sheepish. "Do you want coffee?" Cassy offered, holding up a half-filled pot.

Ethan shook his head with a laugh. "Are you kidding? Harper's aunt loaded us up with cranberry orange bread and massive lattes—"

Robin elbowed him sharply, her eyes flashing with purpose. "Ethan, focus." She turned back to us, voice steady. "We need to tell you what we found out."

I strode to the murder board, pinning the nurse's photo in place. "And you'll want to hear this, too. That's the nurse who's been sneaking Cara in. Cara's husband is alive," I said, tapping the photo for emphasis.

Robin's eyes widened. "With amnesia, right?"

"What? How'd you know?" I asked, raising an eyebrow.

She gestured toward Ethan. "While we were talking to Cara, she just started crying. I had to take over before he bolted out of the room."

Ethan lifted his hands defensively. "I don't do crying."

Robin shook her head with a smirk. "Anyway, Cara admitted she knew. She's been hiding it out of guilt for not telling us or the police."

"Dexter's aware now," I added.

Cassy leaned in, eyes narrowing at the pinned photo. "But if she's been visiting him at midnight, why the secrecy?"

Robin shrugged. "She wants her money back—claims that's all she wants."

"That's it?" Cassy raised a skeptical eyebrow. "Doesn't add up."

I nodded, my fingers tracing the edge of the photo. "What's this nurse's involvement? Could she be a red herring?"

Ethan laughed. "She doesn't look like a fish to me."

I grinned, shaking my head. "A red herring isn't an actual fish, Ethan. It's a distraction—a clue meant to throw us off the real answer."

Just then, Jenny and Ryan burst through the door, bringing a gust of air and wide grins.

"You're not going to believe what we found out!" Jenny announced, tossing her leather coat and backpack onto the counter.

"Cara's husband is alive?" we all blurted in unison.

Jenny paused, blinking. "Wait, what? No." She exchanged a surprised glance with Ryan. "Lila has a brother—and he's been living here, right in Evergreen Heights."

The room went silent, all eyes widening, as another puzzle piece shifted into place.

CHAPTER 16
WARNINGS AND WHISPERS

"WHAT'S that have to do with the case?" I asked.

"We think he planted himself here to scope out Christmas Tree Forest." Jenny said, as she pulled her phone out of her pocket.

"This is him," she continued, showing us a photo of a man on her phone. "Maybe he killed Elmer and has been hiding out somewhere since then."

"He didn't kill Elmer," I replied.

"How can you be so sure?" Jenny said, getting defensive. She liked having the upper hand and beating everyone to clues. Sometimes that got her, and everyone else, into trouble. Sometimes kidnapped and killed. That is, when she reported the clues as fact on her podcast without having any evidence to back it up.

I bit my tongue. I wanted to ask if she planned on releasing the information before she was sure of its accuracy. But I didn't want to start another fight.

Cassy saved my butt by stating, "Sorry to burst your

investigative bubble, Jenny, but that's Cara's husband and he is in the hospital with amnesia."

"Do you think Cara knows her husband is Lila Weston's brother?" Robin asked.

"She had to know, right?" I added. I moved back over to the murder board. "Can you send that photo to my printer, Jenny?"

"This is so confusing, how do you solve these things?" Ethan asked with wide eyes as he studied the board.

"Alright, I know this list of suspects looks like a cast of thousands," I said, tapping the murder board with the fire poker I'd picked up. "But remember, in every good mystery, chaos is just the stage before clarity. Each name on this list is a thread we're tugging on. And when we start following those threads, the ones that don't belong will unravel on their own."

"Like Danny," Ryan said, making a rare contribution to the investigation. "He didn't kill Elmer, so you moved him from the number one suspect position."

"Yes," I tapped on Danny's photo. "And he didn't mean to push Anora."

"So this is organized crime?" Ethan added.

Jenny and the other college students stifled a giggle, which made them sound like cackling crows in a bag.

I had this feeling that Ethan was smarter than he let on. His love for food and enviable metabolism didn't diminish his intelligence, nor did his aversion to watching a girl cry.

As the rest of The Murder Club continued to snicker, I said, "Explain."

He took the poker from my hand and pointed to the

board. "Well, we need to organize the board first." He pointed to each individual on the board. "You have suspects, but you keep changing them. You have motives, but not all of them are for killing Elmer."

"Oh, he's right. We talked about red herrings, misdirects, and chaos before the clarity, but we aren't organized enough to get any clarity." I studied the picture of the nurse for a moment before taking her down.

"Should we clear the board?" Robin asked.

"Yes?" Ethan said with a sideways glance at me.

I nodded permission and then added, "Tell us what to do, Ethan."

Five minutes later, we'd cleared the board and stacked up the photos in a few piles: "Suspects" and "We don't know what they have to do with the case."

Ethan put the photo of Elmer in the middle. "Now I need some string."

I went upstairs to my bedroom and grabbed the box of yarn I'd purchased to someday knit a sweater. Once downstairs, I set it on the coffee table.

Ethan looked through the box. "I need a different color for each…" he paused. "Do you mind if I set this up and then explain?"

I knew what it was like to not be able to verbalize what I was doing while under pressure, so I said, "Sure, what do you need?"

"I need one person to cut the yarn and hand me things." He scanned our faces. "And not talk."

"That leaves me out," Jenny said.

I was about to volunteer when Robin stepped forward. "I can do it."

So where did the rest of us go? If we went to the

kitchen, we'd still essentially be in the same room. My office/bedroom would be too crowded, not to mention awkward.

"Let's go downstairs," I suggested. "Cassy, grab what's left of the cookies. Jenny, grab some water bottles unless people want more coffee."

"I'm coffeed out," Jake said. I'm sure he was, with Cassy filling his mug every time it got below three-fourths of a cup.

Jake grabbed his laptop off the dining room table and walked over to Robin, who was cutting a length of purple yarn. "Text me when you finish," he whispered like we were attending a funeral instead of sitting in my apartment with a murder board in the middle.

With cookies and water bottles secured, we relocated to the second floor of the bookstore, where we could spread out and relax on leather sofas. Rory led the way, hoping to secure a seat at the feet of someone who spewed a lot of crumbs when they ate. He chose me. I'm the one who spews the crumbs. Thanks, Rory.

———

Twenty minutes later, Robin texted Jake:

Finished. Come up.

As we climbed the stairs to my apartment, I said a quick prayer that Ethan did really have super intelligence. He got teased enough. I didn't want to walk into my apartment to find a murder board with crayon drawings and silly string-like artwork. He'd never live it down. Plus, we'd have to assemble the murder board all over again.

I stared in disbelief at the murder board, pleasantly surprised that the prayers I'd whispered on my way up the stairs came true.

As I surveyed Ethan's version of a murder board, I couldn't help but think of *A Beautiful Mind*. "It's like you've created your own version of Nash's universe," I remarked, recalling a line from the film: "I don't believe in luck. I believe in hard work."

Ethan grinned, his eyes sparkling with excitement. "If I can just channel my inner John Nash, maybe I'll crack this case wide open!"

He picked up the fire poker. "In the middle of the board we have Elmer, the victim, and shooting out from him with different colors of thread are people who had connections to him and how."

"What's that on the bottom?" Jenny asked.

He moved away from the board so she could get the entire view. "That's the timeline of events."

Jake moved closer and studied the timeline. "The day of Elmer's murder?"

"No, that's too narrow-minded," Robin suggested. "Ethan went as far back as when Lila's brother came to town."

"So we aren't just solving Elmer's murder?" Ryan said, folding his arms behind his head and rocking from one foot to another. "This is overwhelming."

"If we *do* discover Cara's husband's connection, and how he got amnesia and all the rest of this -" He waved his arm over the board, including the green pine trees he'd drawn to represent Christmas Tree Forest, "then it's a bonus. But in order to find out who killed Elmer, we need to know how everything and everyone is connected."

I clapped my hands and said, "Great job, Ethan."

He took a bow.

Jake snapped a few photos of the board with his phone. "Dude, I'm going to study this and compile some in-depth research."

"Can you print the research and give us each a copy for our next meeting?" I stifled a yawn. "I don't mean to shut this meeting down if you still want to work, but I've got to get to bed. Five-thirty comes pretty early."

Jake shrugged and pushed his glasses up his nose. "Sure I can compile the research if you can print it, Harper. Copies are expensive at the library."

Jenny snapped some photos of the board. "Just be prepared, people. Harper will deliver the research in sunflower folders."

"Not entirely true," I said.

"No folders this time," Jenny said, as she pocketed her phone.

"I didn't say that." I pretended to study the board before saying. "I bought some new folders. Some black ones with skulls for Robin. Floral pink ones for Cassy."

"And for me?" Jenny asked.

"Just a sec," I said as I moved to the armoire and rifled through a drawer. I pulled out a set of sleek black folders with the words "Top Secret" across the cover.

"Oh, I want one now!" She reached for the folder.

"Nope, not until I have the research to put in them."

I glanced at Ethan and Ryan, who were looking like

Rory did when she didn't get a treat–mopy and puppy dog eyed.

"Guys, don't worry, I'll get you some special folders too. I had to get to know you first."

They both grinned like kindergartners getting their first pair of child-safety scissors.

I thought back to when Jake had brought the messages printed out and in a folder because his mom said old people preferred paper and folders. Although I wasn't old, she was right. I was old-school.

As I closed the drawer, the lights flickered, and a soft, eerie hum filled the room. I froze, glancing around as a chill crept up my spine.

Ethan frowned. "Did anyone else hear that?"

Before I could answer, my phone buzzed with a notification. A new message, no name, just an anonymous number:

Stop digging, or you'll be next.

I stared at the screen, my heart pounding. Whoever this was, they were watching us. And they didn't want us to find the truth.

CHAPTER 17

BREAKING POINT

I SHOWED the text to the group.

Jake reached for the phone. "Mind if I take a look?"

While he fiddled with the phone, another text came through.

"It's Zoe," he said. He handed the phone back. I read the text aloud:

> Just a heads up—it's totally normal for the power lines to hum and for the lights to flicker a bit after a snowstorm. Ice can build up on the lines, which makes them hum and sometimes causes lights to blink if there's a tiny disruption in the power. It's just the storm's leftovers, so no ghosts here —promise! 😌

I texted back:

> Thanks, how did you know?

Zoe:

> I'm downstairs in the stockroom, taking
> inventory.
>
> Let me know if you want me to grab
> some extra flashlights for the
> bookstore, just in case! ☺

Phew! I put a hand over my heart and willed it to slow down to a normal rhythm. The bad news was someone was threatening me by phone. The good news is they weren't ghosts in control of the building.

While Jake promised to follow up on the text and where it originated from, Jenny snapped a photo of it. "We are on the right track!" She held her hand up for a high five, which I didn't reciprocate.

Being on the right track was dangerous. It meant someone was watching. If someone was watching, Jenny and I were in danger once again, along with the rest of The Murder Club.

I called Dexter after everyone left, filling him in on the note Jenny had received, and sending him both a screenshot of the note and the text.

There was a huff from his end, followed by three exact seconds of silence. Finally, he said, "Why didn't you tell me about the typed note earlier?"

"I actually came back out to the car to tell you, but…" I hesitated.

"But I kissed you instead," he finished, a hint of frustration slipping into his voice.

"Yes! And who follows up that kind of kiss with, 'Oh, by the way, Jenny Murder got a typed note that ties into the case'?" I asked, fighting to sound reasonable.

"Real investigators, that's who. Not mystery writers posing as them," he shot back, his tone tight with barely concealed irritation.

His words stung, bringing an ache I hadn't expected. I thought we'd finally made progress. Now, here we were again, back to doubting and dismissing. Was our relationship destined to be a constant back-and-forth, a game of *she can, she can't*?

I bit my tongue, staying silent.

Dexter took my silence as surrender. "That's it. No more investigating. And disband The Murder Club."

I took a steadying breath. "Is that an order from the police department or from you?"

"Me," he replied, almost defiantly.

"Then I'm ignoring it."

I hung up before he could respond.

———

With the roads clear, the power outages and humming lines a distant memory, everything got back to normal. The students were busy with classes. Story hour was back in full swing, with some very excited kiddos who you'd think were snowbound for months instead of days.

Today was Elmer's funeral, which had been postponed due to the storm. The whole town of Evergreen Heights would be there, including me, The Murder Club, and Jenny Murder.

I hoped I wouldn't run into Dexter there. He had no

real reason to come unless he was investigating, but since he shot down my theories and still had Danny in custody, convinced it was him, why would he attend? He did know Elmer from the Christmas Tree Forest Campground, so maybe their connection would convince him to attend.

Why was I spending so much time thinking about what Dexter would or wouldn't do? If he came to the funeral, I would do what any rational adult with adequate social skills would do. I would ignore him completely.

Edgar, clad in a black overcoat, joined me on the sidewalk as I walked to the funeral home. He stuck out an elbow, and I linked arms with him.

"So, I did the evaluation on Jenny's brother," Edgar said as we walked briskly down the street.

I stepped over an icy patch on the sidewalk and glanced over at him. "And?"

"He's a great kid. Solid," he replied, adjusting his scarf against the biting wind. "I don't see any reason why he can't intern for your father."

I raised an eyebrow, catching a glimmer of mischief in his eye. "You're giving me the short answer, aren't you?"

He chuckled, nodding. "Yes, yes I am. I sent the full report to your father. And I had Dr. Dennis interview him too, just to be sure I didn't miss anything."

"Oh, good," I said, a surge of relief in my voice. "Jenny will be glad to hear it."

Edgar tucked his gloved hands into his coat pockets as he continued. "Your father is interviewing him tomorrow via Zoom. I was hoping we could set it up at the Cozy Corner. I want to give him a bit of coaching beforehand."

"Of course," I replied, dodging another slick spot on the sidewalk and looking up at him with a smile. "We can use the second floor. I'll let Zoe know to keep it clear."

"Thank you," he said, giving a nod of appreciation.

"Thank *you* for doing this," I replied, the gratitude genuine in my tone. "Is he arriving tonight?"

Edgar nodded. "Jenny says his bus gets in around eight."

We finished our conversation just as we arrived at Serenity Pines Funeral Home. The foyer was crowded with people trying to enter the coat room and remove their coats, hats, gloves, and scarfs.

Edgar stopped to talk to a few of The Classics. I slipped through the throng of people, muttering "excuse me" exactly five times before finally emerging into the sitting room adjacent to the viewing room, where I spotted Aunt Mary.

"Aunt Mary," I called, waving as I crossed the room.

She dabbed at her eye with a tissue and managed a small wave back, still clutching the tissue. I took a seat in the wingback chair next to her, leaning forward a little. "Are you okay?" I asked softly.

She sniffed and glanced down at the crumpled tissue. "I can't help thinking this is my fault," she murmured, her voice trembling.

"It's not," I assured her, giving her shoulder a gentle squeeze. "What happened to Elmer had nothing to do with you."

She sniffed again and cleared her throat. "Cara says her husband is in the hospital with amnesia."

That was a sudden turn. But if talking about Cara's drama got Aunt Mary's mind off Elmer's murder, I'd happily go along with it. "Yes, he is," I said, nodding. "She's visited him a few times."

Aunt Mary pressed her lips together and shook her head. "She just wanted to know where her money was so she wouldn't have to sell," she said, her voice tinged with disappointment.

I sighed. "I know, but he doesn't even know who he is."

"Well," Aunt Mary muttered, folding her arms, "I guess she'll never find her money. But Lila and Coldwater Corp are still willing to buy her property, so at least she won't have to move."

"It's not really what I wanted," Cara's voice chimed in from behind me.

I turned, startled, as she appeared from the shadows. "Oh, Cara, join us," I said, waving her over. "I didn't realize you were there."

Cara offered a quick, apologetic smile. "Hey, Harper. Sorry to eavesdrop." She extracted herself from behind the chair, stepped through the tight space, and settled into the loveseat across from me. "But I'm kind of laying low right now."

I leaned forward, curious. "Why is that?"

She shifted her weight, glancing over her shoulder before leaning in close, as if she were about to divulge a guarded secret. She whispered, "Because my husband is Lila's brother. He took my money, doesn't remember who he is or where the money is."

She leaned back and took a deep breath before continuing. "So that gives me motive, and that Detective boyfriend of yours hauled me in for questioning earlier this morning." She stood and paced back and forth. "I'm a suspect."

"But why?" Aunt Mary asked.

"Because before my husband disappeared, I told him I wasn't selling the five hundred acres to anyone."

"I don't understand…" I started, but my words were drowned out as the music of *How Great Thou Art* faded from the intercom, replaced by a clear announcement:

"Ladies and gentlemen, we kindly ask for your attention. We are gathered here today to honor the life and legacy of Professor Elmer Rockwood. A dedicated educator at Evergreen University, Elmer inspired countless students and colleagues with his passion for forestry and conservation. Throughout his distinguished career, he received numerous awards for his contributions to environmental science and education. As we celebrate his memory, let us take a moment to reflect on the impact he made in his field and in our lives. The service will begin shortly. Thank you for being here to honor his legacy."

I fell silent, absorbing the weight of the moment.

We filed into the viewing room and took a seat as the funeral director took the podium in front of the casket." Welcome, friends of Elmer Rockwood. I speak on the behalf of our dearly departed friend when I say thank you for being here to honor his life and legacy." He stopped and straightened his toupee, which had slipped and threatened to cover his left eye. "Elmer had requested his funeral be held at Christmas Tree Forest, but the snowstorm has obviously ruled against us. For those of you who are close to him, and care to brave the snowdrifts, Fiona will be holding a short service for him on the Hemlock Trail at noon tomorrow." He stepped back from the podium. "Pastor Samuel, if you could take over."

Pastor rose and replaced the funeral director at the podium. "Welcome to this celebration of Elmer's life and legacy. Although Elmer was a regular church attender, he told me that the woods were the place he really worshiped God. When he heard the call of a Whippoorwill, late one night from his campsite at Christmas Tree Forest, he called me on the phone to share. It was midnight."

A titter of laughter rippled through the audience.

From my vantage point in the audience, I had a clear view of Fiona's back, in the front row next to some of The Classics, including Edgar. I turned and glanced behind me. College students took up the last row, including my Murder Club. I didn't see Dexter, which made me breathe a sigh of relief.

"Is this seat taken?"

I swiveled to my left to see who had asked.

"Dexter," I hissed. "I'm not talking to you."

"I'm not here to talk to you. I'm here to attend a funeral." He motioned to the chair. "Do you mind?"

Aunt Mary leaned over me. "Dexter, have a seat." Then she put her finger to her lips. "Shh."

The funeral was short. I appreciated the fact that Pastor didn't paint some fake glossy picture of Elmer's life. Not that he was a bad guy. He wasn't. But when someone dies, it's not the time to pretend they lived sinless lives. Pastor ended with the scripture:

> *John 14:1-3:* "Do not let your hearts be troubled. You believe in God; believe also in me. My Father's house has many rooms; if that were not so, would I have told you that I am going there to prepare a place for you?"

I thought of Elmer in heaven. The place he'd like prepared for him was a forest. I hoped he had a big backyard full of hemlocks, oaks, maples, and every kind of bird. I didn't know if my thoughts were theologically sound, but that didn't matter. God knew Elmer. He would take care of him. Another thought sprang to mind. Backyard. I needed to talk to Cara.

After we sang a hymn, Pastor released us and invited us to join him at the town hall for refreshments. Some people lingered at the casket, talking about their memories of Elmer, including Aunt Mary. I was alone with Dexter. Kind of. The room was packed with people, the aisles jammed so tightly that moving felt impossible. I stood frozen, my chest tightening as the familiar agoraphobic dread crept in, making me feel utterly stuck and out of control. Why didn't Dexter flash his badge and clear out the aisle? It was too crowded in here. My breath came in short gasps. I fell back into my seat and put my head between my legs, like Edgar had taught me. The world spun and darkness closed in on me. I slid off the chair and with a thud hit the red carpet.

Voices drifted toward me, muffled and warped, as though coming from behind a thick wall.

"Call 911."

"No, don't."

"We just need to get her home."

Strong arms lifted me, and I sank into something cold and hard—a chair with metal bars and wheels. The chill of the seat shocked me back to a flicker of awareness.

Outside. I sucked in a deep breath of frigid air, the sharpness clearing my head just enough for me to lift it slightly. The chair sped down the sidewalk, my body jostling with each bump, until we hit a patch of ice, and the wheels spun, sending us in a dizzying circle. I found myself facing the person pushing me.

Dexter's eyes were fixed on me, worry etched deep into his face.

Edgar followed close behind, guiding Aunt Mary as they hurried to keep pace.

As Dexter steadied the chair, his eyes held a look I couldn't shake—something between frustration and pity. I swallowed hard, his earlier words echoing in my mind.

Maybe he was right. Maybe I wasn't cut out for this, for any of it. Not with my mind constantly warring against itself, my agoraphobia clawing at me, my senses overloaded at every turn.

How could I ever trust myself to see this through?

CHAPTER 18
FALLS, FRAUD, AND FRAMED FOR MURDER

I SPENT two days in bed, under my weighted blanket. I refused any visitors except Aunt Mary, Edgar and Dexter. Since I'd requested no visitors, Dexter respected my wishes by sitting downstairs and talking with Mary and Edgar when he stopped by exactly five times. I kind of regretted not allowing him to come to my room and sit beside the bed like Edgar did, to be a comforting, calming presence.

Aunt Mary called my mother and filled her in. I hoped to heaven she didn't hop on a plane and come. Who was I kidding? There would be no publicity for her to revel in, like the week of Thanksgiving or when Aunt Mary was accused of murder while filming her show Sell It Or Stay. She'd stay put.

I Facetimed with my mother and father the second day I was in bed.

"Harper, do something with that hair," Mother said. "Wash your face and pull yourself together." The mascara that I'd worn to Elmer's funeral had settled into the dark circles under my eyes and run down each eye, giving me the appearance of a sad clown. The Face-Time meeting was the first time I'd seen my face since putting makeup on for the funeral. "I'm sending you some moisturizer and if you're going to lounge around in bed, you might as well have the appropriate loungewear." Mother stood and moved away from my father's laptop. "Pepita," she yelled.

"Scarlett, you're yelling in my ear," my father said.

My mother's heels clicked on the marble floor in their Paris apartment as she went in search of Pepita, who I knew would be in charge of shipping the moisturizer and loungewear to me.

My father was never sure what to say when I had a meltdown or shutdown or whatever my body did. So he talked about other things.

"So that kid you recommended. I interviewed him yesterday."

"Oh, that's right," I sat up straighter, fluffing two pillows to support me. "How did that go?" Jenny's brother, Brian, was here. I missed meeting him.

"It went well. He's a smart kid. He knows his art, and he's good with numbers." He leaned back in his espresso-brown high-backed office chair and folded his arms in front of him. "I think he'll be a good fit. I'm flying him here."

"There? I thought he'd work stateside for you."

"I'd like to train him myself." He smiled.

"Dad, this is Jenny Murders brother. He can't afford a place in Paris."

As I lay in bed, my dad's face flickering on my

screen, I tried to focus on his familiar voice, but my mind kept drifting. I imagined the Pont de Bir-Hakeim with Jenny's brother huddled under those arches, shaking and begging for bread. The fear gnawed at me —if he couldn't get his life on track, would he end up like that? Just another lost soul in the city's shadows, slipping further away from everyone who cared? I shook my head. My literary mind was getting the better of me. I'd suddenly gone all *Les Misérables*.

My mother's face popped back on the screen, blurred because she'd gotten too close. "I sent some suits to that lovely young man, Brian." She puckered her lips. "He couldn't exactly fly on a plane in that tattered one he was wearing for the interview."

"Scarlett, do you mind?" my father said.

"And he's staying in your room," my mother added as she backed away from the computer and clacked out of the room.

My room? Since when had I had a room? I hadn't been to Paris since I was twelve. Although I was relieved that Brian was going to have a place to stay, I wondered if he was ready for my parents. They were definitely more challenging than the drill sergeant at the academy Brian had just escaped from.

"He'll be flying here tomorrow," my father was saying. I'm sure he said other things, but my body was tuning out. I was checking out.

"Dad, I need to rest," I said.

He leaned forward, his hand hovering over the keyboard. Ready to click out of the meeting. "Of course. Are you sure you don't want the doctor I recommended to come check on you? He's world-renowned."

"No dad, Aunt Mary is taking care—"

He clicked out before I finished the sentence.

I slid the laptop off my lap and onto my bedside table and fell asleep.

When I woke, Aunt Mary was sitting beside my bed with Rory at her feet.

"Harper, you're awake."

"Barely."

"Detective Dexter arrested Cara for Elmer's murder." She said "detective" in a disgusted tone.

"What?" I sat up. That woke me up.

"You've got to help her. She didn't do this."

"I'm not on the case anymore." I pulled my weighted blanket off and swung my legs around. I stood and braced myself on her knee. "I have to pee."

"Do you need help?" she asked. Rory stood and nuzzled the back of my knee.

I turned and patted him on the head. "No, just keep Rory here so he doesn't knock me over."

As I padded my way to the bathroom, shuffling along like a geriatric one hundred-year-old, Aunt Mary added, "Your Murder Club kids have been here twice and Zoe won't let them come up."

"There is no Murder Club," I said as I shut the door to the bathroom.

Aunt Mary didn't stop talking.

"So Danny isn't being charged with murder anymore. Anora's awake. She's going on and on about meeting Elmer the day he died. The doctor says she's not entirely coherent. But she said what happened was an accident. Danny wasn't trying to kill her."

I stood and flushed, pulling my moose-covered

flannel pjs up. I moved to the sink and studied my sad clown face. I turned the water on and waited for it to heat up. I slathered some face wash on and scrubbed with the exfoliating machine Mother had sent me. I rinsed and grabbed a hand towel. My face was now shiny and mascara-free. My little gray cells, as Hercule Poirot aptly named them, were waking up.

"Why did Dexter arrest Cara?"

I rehung the hand towel and exited the bathroom.

Aunt Mary was smiling. "I knew you'd want to know. You can't stand not knowing the answers. You're good at this sleuthing stuff."

"Not according to Dexter," I said, folding my arms and giving her a look.

"Oh pooh, he's just worried about you," Aunt Mary replied, dismissively waving a hand. "He's not as good as you are at this stuff."

I raised an eyebrow, incredulous. "How could you say that?"

She leaned in, a mischievous glint in her eye. "Who got the text warning them to back off?"

I sighed. "I did."

She nodded smugly. "You see? You always get close enough to the killer to make them nervous. Meanwhile, Detective Dexter is off chasing red herrings. That's what you call them, right?"

"Yes," I muttered, shaking my head. "Thank you for the vote of confidence. But you still haven't told me why he arrested Cara."

Aunt Mary's eyes sparkled with a secret. "I thought I'd let her tell you."

My head snapped up. "She's here?"

"Yes. She's downstairs with Edgar," she paused, letting that sink in, "and The Murder Club." Another pause. "And Jenny."

I glanced down at my flannel pajamas, wrinkled and worn from two days straight. "Can I take a shower?"

She gave me an amused smile, already pulling out her phone. "Yes, I'll order you some food and have it delivered. Now, do you want to go downstairs, or would you prefer everyone come up here?"

I thought about it for a minute. One, I didn't want to endure the stares and whispers that were sure to buzz around me like bees in the cafe and bookstore. Whispers such as "She doesn't look like she's crazy, but one never knows." Okay, that was my mother's voice. Even so, well-meaning or not, there would be questions, stares, and whispers. Two, the carefully constructed murder board was in my apartment. I wanted to see Cara's reaction to it.

As I headed to my closet, I said, "Up here. Give me fifteen minutes."

Rory joined me and nuzzled a dress, a spice-colored ribbed sweater dress, and then a pair of brown boots.

"Ordered your food," she called before sticking her head in the closet. "Come on, Rory, Aunt Mary is going to take you out."

She laughed when she saw Rory sticking his nose in a pair of brown boots. "Is he still picking out your clothes?"

"Let's face it Aunt Mary, he does a better job than my mother." I held up the sweater dress.

"That's true," she said with a chuckle.

Fifteen minutes later, I was showered and dressed.

Aunt Mary brought up the promised food, along with Rory, Cara, and The Murder Club.

Jenny plopped down on the sectional. "I had to record a bonus episode because you were incapacitated."

"Sorry to inconvenience you." I threw a pillow at her.

She caught the pillow. "Hey, thanks for helping Brian. Really. I mean it. This internship is life-changing for him."

I replied, "Does he know my mother plans to dress him for the flight and probably for the rest of his life?"

"Harper, your parents are not only giving him a job, they're flying him to Paris, to live with them. He's ecstatic."

Aunt Mary set my food on the table and beckoned me over. The Murder Club members hovered at the island.

"I'll make coffee," Cassy offered.

"She's fine," Robin said to Ethan and Ryan.

"She's not broken?" Ryan whispered.

So the whispers had sneaked up here to my apartment.

Cara joined Jenny by the sectional.

"Robin, come here." I motioned her toward me.

She walked from the island to the dining room table. "I want you to observe Cara's reaction to the murder board."

"Will do, but I'm pretty sure Jenny's got you covered."

I glanced over. Jenny had left her place at the sectional and stood beside Cara as she moved to study the board. Jenny's phone was poised and ready to record.

I ate my bacon avocado burger and sweet potato fries quickly so I could talk to Cara before Jenny freaked her out to the point that she fled the apartment.

While the students busied themselves with coffee and the baked goods Zoe had sent up, Cara joined me at the table.

I wiped my mouth and asked, "How are you doing?"

"You mean how am I doing because I'm the number one suspect in Elmer's murder and I'm at the top of your murder board?"

"Yes," I answered.

Ignoring the question, Cara continued, "I'm sorry. You've been sick since you collapsed at the funeral. How are you?"

"I'm fine. Really. Aunt Mary said you wanted to talk to me?" I wasn't going to explain my condition, or whatever you called it. Autism. Sensory Overload. Shut down.

"I started to tell you at the funeral home." She picked up a napkin and folded it before she continued. "My husband is Lila's brother and a con man. He changed his name before he married me."

"Oh," I said, my mouth staying in the "o" formation.

The students joined us and Cassy handed Cara a cup of coffee and a plate with a cranberry orange muffin on it.

"Mind if I record?" Jenny asked.

"Will it help my case?"

"I think so," I patted her hand. "As long as Jenny

doesn't edit or add important details," I said, giving Jenny the warning look Aunt Mary used on me when I was about to cross the line.

"Okay," Cara said and wrapped her hands around her coffee mug. "Shall I repeat what I just said?"

"Please," Jenny said, as she set her mic in the middle of the table. "Everyone, try to not clink your mugs and saucers." She began in her podcaster voice:

[Jenny Murder]: *Welcome to Crimecaster, Cara! Thank you for being here.*

[Cara]: Thanks, Jenny. I'm glad to set the record straight.

[Jenny]: *Let's start with your husband. He went by Nathan, but you learned that wasn't his real name. What happened there?*

[Cara]: That's right. He introduced himself as Nathan, but his real name is Luther Weston. He's actually a developer who planned to con me into selling 500 acres next to Christmas Tree Forest. I only discovered his true identity and intentions after he'd drained my bank account and left me in debt.

[Jenny]: *Did he just vanish after taking your money?*

[Cara]: He tried to. But when he fled, the assumption is he tripped on a root along Hemlock Trail in Christmas Tree Forest and took a pretty bad fall. A hiker was on the trail, found him and called 911. Nathan ended up in the hospital with amnesia.

[Jenny]: *And you didn't find this out right away?*

[Cara]: No. No, the elderly 911 caller was confused about the identity of the man he'd found, mistakenly thinking it was his childhood friend. His memory

issues left the paramedics with little to go on. He couldn't provide a name, only repeating that he'd found a young man in the woods. The details were muddled—one moment he'd insist it was someone he knew, the next he seemed unsure if the person was even alive when he found him. So for a long time, I had no idea where my husband was or why he'd disappeared so suddenly.

[Jenny]: *That must have left you in a tough position, especially financially.*

[Cara]: It did. There was no way I could keep up with the debt he'd left behind, so I had to make a choice. Harper's Aunt Mary has this show called Sell It Or Stay, and the rule was that if I couldn't afford the upgrades needed, I'd have to sell the land. So, with no other options, I was afraid I'd have to put it up for sale once the renovations were completed.

[Jenny]: *And then Elmer was killed, and you were accused of his murder. How did that happen?*

[Cara]: Because no one knew where Nathan was, only that he had disappeared. Rumors swirled. But the idea that I'd harm Elmer didn't make sense. He was on my side, just as determined to protect Christmas Tree Forest as I was. We shared the same goal, and I had no reason to kill him—if anything, his support made him an ally in a fight we both cared deeply about.

[Jenny]: *What's next for you, Cara?*

[Cara]: I'm focused on clearing my name and moving forward. I still believe that something good can come from all of this.

Jenny clicked off the recording and grabbed the mic.

"That's a wrap. Good job, Cara. I'm going to go edit and prep this to release this evening."

As Jenny packed up her equipment, Cara's phone buzzed with a message. She glanced down, her face going pale. "She knows we're talking," she whispered.

CHAPTER 19
TERROR IN THE TREE LAB

CARA RUSHED OUT of the apartment before I could ask who *she* was. Jenny followed with her podcast equipment on her back. The rest of us sat together in stunned silence.

"I've never been on a podcast before," Ethan said, finally breaking the silence.

"I don't think you can count that as being on a podcast," Ryan said.

"Who do you think *she* is?" Robin asked.

"Lila," Cassy said with conviction. "Maybe Danny covered for his mom. She murdered Elmer."

"Where did you come up with that?" I asked.

"It was on Jenny's Crimecaster bonus episode. 'Overlooked Suspects'."

"Oh, I'll have to listen to that one."

I wanted more than anything to get back into bed. But The Murder Club was here and looking to me to clear Cara's name and find the real killer.

"Let's catch up on what we know." I stood and

picked up my mug. "First, get a refill if you need it, and let's meet at the murder board."

A few minutes later, we were seated in the dining room chairs in a semicircle in front of the murder board. "Jake, what did you find out about the text I got when the electricity hummed?"

"Burner phone," he said. "I couldn't trace it. Whoever used it already discarded it."

"So a dead end," Robin said.

"What about the typed note?" I continued.

"Well, Sage said Jenny had mucked up all the evidence she could have gotten from it," he said and pushed his glasses up.

"What about the typewriter?" Ethan asked.

"Good question, Ethan," Robin said.

"There are two in the public library and one in the college library. Only one matches the typeset of the note. A Smith-Corona Sterling right across the street in the public library."

I smiled. "That's good news."

"Not really. Public library." Jake continued. "Yes, I talked to the librarian. She said the local elementary school's fourth grade teacher encouraged her class to type their spelling words for practice."

"So. No fingerprints," Ryan offered.

"Lots of smudged sticky fingerprints," Jake answered.

Ethan stood and went to the board. "Not to change the subject but those seem like dead ends. If Cassy is right and Lila texted Cara, then we need to dig deeper into the corruption issue." He pointed to the orange yarn stretching from Elmer to Lila. He grabbed a dry erase marker and added Luther's name.

Robin stood. "So it's a family of con artists. Danny cons people by making them feel as if he is on their side. Luther changes his name and cons women out of their money."

I folded my hands in my lap and pressed my feet into the floor to ground myself. "I'd love to talk to Anora and see what else Elmer had in the folder."

"I'll contact the hospital and see if she is awake," Aunt Mary said from the reading chair in the corner.

She stood and picked her phone up before going out into the hallway to place the call.

"Back to the Weston family. I'm pretty sure they're training Lila's niece to join the family business," I said.

"What do you mean?" Cassy asked.

"When Dexter and I went to question Lila, her niece Fredicka was pretending to be the maid, which she was terrible at, but she made some excuse about trying out for a play," I said.

"Lila's niece. So Luther's daughter?" Ethan added her to the board.

"Do you think Cara knows?" Cassy asked.

"I don't think it matters at this point. The more important thing is getting Cara's name cleared. Hopefully Jenny's podcast will help."

We had nothing but dead ends, and I was fading quickly.

Aunt Mary breezed back in with her phone in the air. "Anora is awake and she wants to talk to you, Harper! And Jenny!"

I stood. "Oh, she's okay?"

"She's a little groggy, but otherwise, she's fine. She said she wants to talk to you before the police so you need to get over there." She picked up her coat and mine off the hooks. "Come on, let's go."

"What do you want us to do?" Robin said.

"Can you stay here and keep Rory company? But more importantly, see what else you can find out about the Weston family."

"On it," Jake said.

———

Aunt Mary leaned forward in the driver's seat and sped to the hospital like we were fleeing from a crime scene instead of going to interview a potential witness who wasn't going anywhere.

"Be careful, there are still some icy spots."

"We need to beat the detective there," she said as she pressed the accelerator.

Ten minutes later, we hopped off the elevator on Anora's floor. No sign of Dexter yet. When the nurse gave us Anora's room number, she pointed. "Room 201. It's open. She has a visitor already." She pointed to the room closest to the nurse's station.

I guess he did beat us here. Then I heard the distinct sound of two women arguing. Anora and ... I recognized the other voice. Fiona.

Aunt Mary pulled me to right outside of the door and I grabbed her arm and shushed her. "Wait," I mouthed. I peeked in. Fiona was standing beside the hospital bed.

She froze. "Elmer was my friend," Fiona challenged.

"He was mine too. Calm down Fiona, I'm not arguing with you." Anora replied.

"He wouldn't want his research to fall into the wrong hands," Fiona countered.

"You're right."

"So you'll give it to me?"

"I don't have it," Anora said. "I must have lost it when I fell over the snowbank."

Fiona opened the closet and searched. "Surely you have a copy?"

"No. I'm sorry. That's the only copy I had."

Fiona shut the closet. "I'm sorry. I'm just upset," she explained. "I shouldn't have yelled at you. My friend is dead and his research is missing." She patted Anora on the hand and added, "Hope you feel better soon."

Fiona picked up her leather backpack and turned for the door. I pulled Aunt Mary back five feet and proceeded to act as if we were walking down the hallway toward Anora's room.

"Oh, hello Fiona," Aunt Mary said. "How is Anora?"

Fiona smiled. "She's on the mend." There was something about the smile. Like the cat who'd just swallowed a mouse kind of smile.

Fiona gave me a quick wave and kept moving down the hallway toward the elevator.

"Well, that was interesting…"

"What? She's upset about Elmer and his research disappearing," Aunt Mary said, as we knocked on Anora's door.

"Is she though?"

"Hello…" Aunt Mary said and paused to give her a quick wave.

Anora tightened her robe and patted her bedhead hair. "Oh, Mary, come in. Did you bring Harper?"

"Here," I said.

She glanced to the open door. "And Jenny? The Crimecaster?"

I moved to the bed and smiled. "I texted her on the way here. She should be here any minute."

"I'm here," Jenny slid in the doorway. "Let's get this started. I have it on good authority Detective Dexter will be here any moment."

She pulled out her phone and pressed record.

Anora took the signal and began.

"Danny didn't mean for me to fall. I'm not pressing charges. But I wanted you to know that folder didn't have all of Elmer's research."

I opened my mouth to say "but you just said," then I realized I'd be telling on Aunt Mary and me for eavesdropping so I closed my mouth without saying a word.

"I told Fiona I lost all the research, but Elmer had it all backed up on his computer. I helped him with that. He wasn't too keen on computers."

"But his laptop was missing from his home office."

"That's because he asked me to hide his things in my portable lab."

"Your RV at the campsite?" I couldn't help myself. I had to ask.

"Yes, but I can't get to it. They're keeping me here for a few more days for observation. I want you two to go secure it."

Jenny and I looked at each other. "Should we go now?" she asked.

"The sooner the better," Anora said. "There's a good chance that Lila or one of her family members already got to it."

Jenny clicked the button on her phone, ending the recording.

"Let's go," I said.

"I'll stay here with Anora," Aunt Mary said.

"Jenny," Anora said. "Don't release any of that info yet. Save it. We don't want to tip our hand."

"Of course," Jenny said.

Why couldn't Jenny respond to Sage and me that way, instead of giving a smart retort and doing the opposite of what we asked? This wasn't the time to bring that up. I needed Jenny. We rushed down the hall to the elevator. I pushed the button and Jenny asked, "You okay to do this? I mean after the last few days…"

The elevator doors slid open with a soft ding, and there stood Dexter, his gaze sharp and unyielding as he stepped in between us.

"Harper, you're…"

I could finish the sentence he couldn't.

"Out of bed," I said.

"I was going to say, looking well."

"Sure you were Poindexter." Jenny said.

"You're leaving?" he asked.

"We have an errand to run for Anora," I said as Jenny and I stepped in the elevator and she pushed the close button three times.

As the elevator doors closed, I felt Dexter's inquisitive eyes on me. He didn't say a word, but he was clearly miffed that I didn't give him a clear answer.

"So as I was saying, you're okay to do this?" Jenny asked.

"We're just going to the campground to pick up a laptop and some papers."

"Did you write down the safe combination?"

"Of course. Easy-peasy. We'll be home in an hour," I said, more to reassure myself than her.

"What was your good authority?" I added.

"What?"

"You said you had it on good authority that Dexter was coming."

"I saw him pull into the parking garage." She giggled.

———

Ten minutes later, we pulled into the Christmas Tree Forest parking lot. It was only a short walk to Anora's lab/RV. I prayed we didn't run into people who wanted to chat on the way. I wanted to get in and get out as quickly as possible. I recited the combination to the safe under my breath as we approached the RV.

"I'll go in and open the safe," I said. "You stay out here and stand watch."

"Stand watch? For what? No one's here."

"For the bear," I said as I opened the door and slipped in.

I found the safe in the high-tech lab behind a topical map of Christmas Tree Forest and typed in the code. I pulled out the laptop and the folders of what I assumed were Elmer's research. My back was to the door.

Jenny shrieked. Did a bear really get her? I thought they hibernated. Before running out to check on her, I thought it prudent to peek out the window first.

Fiona? Was that a gun?

"Harper, I'll take that laptop and the folders. Now or your friend dies."

A cold sweat prickled down my spine as Fiona's icy voice cut through the air.

"Harper, now." Her gun was trained squarely on Jenny, who stood frozen, terror in her eyes.

I tightened my grip on the laptop, my mind racing. One wrong move, and I could lose everything—my life and Jenny's.

CHAPTER 20
THE WRONG DECISION

I SHOVED the computer and folders into a cubby behind a field microscope and closed the safe.

"Ummm. I can't get the safe open," I said, trying to buy some time.

"Don't play games with me, Harper. Everyone in town knows you're the smartest—you probably pieced this together ages ago," Fiona spat, slamming her fists against the side of the RV with a force that shook it. There was raw anger in her eyes, the kind that simmered and then boiled over. It was nothing like Dexter's cool, calculating control. He could unravel a case thread by thread without breaking a sweat. Fiona, though—she was all rage and fire, ready to explode without a second thought. I wished I had answered Dexter completely back at the hospital. He could be here, calming my nerves and handling Fiona. Only he wasn't coming.

"I'm submitting that research. Most days Elmer couldn't tell a cerulean warbler from a cardinal."

I pretended to fiddle with the safe. "I'm trying. Please don't hurt Jenny."

I didn't bring my phone, so there was no way to contact anyone. I'd made the mistake of telling Aunt Mary and Anora not to tell Detective Dexter where we were going. The campground was deserted so no one would hear a gunshot. Or find our bodies until the snow cleared.

"You can come out," Fiona said.

"Let me try the safe one more time, please," I begged.

I knew two things. One, if I handed Fiona all the research, she would kill us. Two, if I didn't get the research for her, she would kill us. My only option was to stall until help came. But help wasn't coming, was it?

"Mind if I turn on the heater? My hands are getting cold."

Fiona said nothing, so I set the thermostat on heat mode and turned it up to seventy while thinking of other things I could do to stall.

"Why don't you come in and get out of the cold?" I suggested. "And tell us about your research."

The RV door swung open and Fiona shoved Jenny up the stairs. She motioned to the table with benches. Jenny slid in one side and I slid in the other. Fiona's normally tame braids were unraveling, giving her the look of a wild animal.

"Aunt Mary said she thought Elmer was suffering from dementia," I said. "That's why she took him to the hospital after the town hall meeting incident."

I glanced at Jenny, who wore a look of terror and determination. We'd been here before, at death's door, together. Jenny nodded to Fiona's boots. L.L.Bean Trekkers.

"Yes, we found the bird together hiking on some of the higher peaks of the park. We sighted one, and to prove the nest was there, I climbed the sugar maple and used a drone to take photos of it."

She slammed the gun down hard on the table, accidentally pulling the trigger. My heart hammered as the bullet seared past, close enough to feel the heat as it whipped through my hair and lodged in the cabinet beside me. I couldn't breathe, couldn't move, pinned there by shock and the wild look in Fiona's eyes. She was unhinged. No, worse—she was gone, like I was looking at a stranger wearing her face.

"Are you insane?" I managed, my voice tight and trembling. I slid back and huddled against the wall of the RV. I needed distance, anything to keep me grounded, anything to keep me safe. "You could have killed me!"

But it was like I wasn't even there. Her gaze was glassy, somewhere far away, focused on something only she could see. I swallowed hard, my hands gripping the edge of the table to keep from shaking. Fiona had always been calm and kind, but this persona...this was something else entirely.

"Fiona..." I said, softer now, hoping to reach her. "You need help. This isn't you."

Something flickered in her eyes for a second—recognition, maybe even guilt. But then it was gone, that fractured expression settling back over her like a mask. I felt a shiver crawl up my spine.

I had to get out. But not without Jenny.

I took a few deep breaths and, with my hands trembling, I picked up the coffee pot. "How about I make us some coffee and you can finish your story?"

"First, get the computer and files out of the safe."

"Okay." I stepped back into the lab section and pulled them out from behind the field microscope, rummaging around for something, anything I could use as a weapon. I found a tranq gun and slipped it into my coat pocket.

I took the few steps back to the living quarters section and held the laptop up. "Now let her go," I said. "Or you're not getting this." With bravado I didn't possess, I turned to the sink and turned the water on. I held the files and laptop dangerously close to the stream of water.

"You wouldn't." She jabbed the gun into Jenny's side. "I need her."

I stepped back. "For what?"

"She's going to record a podcast sharing my side of the story." She held up Jenny's phone, which she must have taken from her outside.

I looked to Jenny for an answer. She nodded in assent. Of course she would. With a gun held to her head or any other part of her body. Jenny would sacrifice her life for the story.

She handed Jenny the phone and pulled the gun out of her ribs.

Jenny breathed a sigh of relief and opened an app on her phone.

"No funny business. No texting anyone. I just want you to record my story."

Fiona turned to me. "You can make the coffee, Harper."

Something smacked against the top of the RV with a solid, echoing *whump*. The impact rattled through the thin metal, making the whole vehicle shudder. Fiona jumped, her eyes widening as she whipped around, face pale with a mixture of shock and irritation. Her hand flew to her chest, and she let out a shaky breath before muttering, "Just snow."

It was enough time for me to pull the tranq gun out and show Jenny. She shook her head no. I knew what she meant. She wanted the recording first, then I'd have to find an opportunity to shoot Fiona before she killed us both.

I finished making coffee and brought three cups to the table. I sat down across from Fiona so I could tranq her as soon as she gave her full confession on the podcast.

"Do I have your permission to record?" Jenny asked.

"Of course you do, I just told you to, didn't I?"

"Fiona, she has to ask that for legal reasons. She does for every podcast recording," I said, trying to calm her down.

"Let's start with when you found the bird."

Her moss-colored eyes sparkled as she recalled the memory and began. "A flash of blue caught my eye—a warbler, bright as the clear sky, hopping effortlessly through the high canopy. It was a male Cerulean Warbler, his delicate neck band and side streaks a vivid cerulean, perfectly suited for the dappled light filtering through the eastern forests." Fiona looked as if she were in another world, a smile on her face, the crazed look gone.

She continued. "Watching him, my heart sank a little, knowing how rare these sightings had become, how their numbers were dwindling as forests shrank."

It was as if Fiona thought she was directing a wildlife talk at a nature seminar. When was she going to get to the part where Elmer stole the research and she murdered him?

I kicked Jenny under the table.

"And Elmer took your research?" Jenny asked.

"He invited me on a hike one day to show me what he'd found. He said he'd been observing the bird and taking notes for weeks."

When she realized what she'd just said, she back-tracked.

"I mean, you saw Elmer's mental decline first hand. He couldn't remember people from one day to the next."

I shook my head in agreement, at the same time thinking, *gotcha*.

Fiona continued to talk about the research for ten minutes as if it were hers and how she was going to turn it into Evergreen University and finally get the credit for it.

We needed to get to the part where she murdered Elmer.

"I think that's all," she said. She'd said nothing about going to his house, the typed note, the argument, or any of the other loose ends.

Jenny pushed pause on the recording. "Well, I need to get home so I can edit this."

"Oh, no you don't." Crazy Fiona was back.

"Fiona," I said. "Let's face it. You're not going to let either of us go."

"See I said you were the smartest."

"So why don't you answer a few questions?"

I kicked Jenny again. Read my mind, Jenny. Record.

Jenny held the phone under the table and pushed the record button again.

"After I answer your questions, we're going to walk out into the woods and no one will find your bodies until spring."

"You're going to shoot us?" Jenny asked.

"Of course not. I'm terrible with this thing." She waved the gun around. Jenny and I both ducked as she cackled. "I have some Foxglove for both of you. Jenny, set the phone on the table."

Jenny complied, making sure it was screen-side down.

Not poison. I'd had a near death experience with poison before Christmas and I wasn't about to have one again.

"Elmer had all the research," Fiona continued with the assurance and confidence of someone who felt as if her plan was going to work.

"I begged him to let me submit it. He refused."

"So you followed him home from the hospital and killed him?"

"Yes, I did. I didn't want to kill him. I went there to get his laptop. He said he'd given the research to someone for safekeeping."

"And the text?" I recited it from memory.

"Yes, that was to throw you off. I knew Danny

wasn't who he said he was. You saw him call a hemlock a shagbark hickory."

"Nothing is going on with the town council."

"No, just Lila Weston, Luther and their family of con artists."

That was it. I had all I needed. I signaled to Jenny. It was time to tranq Fiona.

Jenny wasn't finished. "The typed note."

"Oh, that was easy enough. The typewriter at the library. The keys were covered with sticky cheesy snack residue, so I knew they were being used often." She stood and grabbed Jenny's arm. "That's enough. Let's go."

"What about the podcast episode?" Jenny asked, as Fiona jerked her to her feet.

"Publish it."

"Right now?"

"Yes, right now."

Jenny turned her phone over, and in a split second Fiona realized she was being recorded. She lunged for the phone, releasing her grip on Jenny.

The phone slid across the table toward me. I grabbed it and ran to the back of the RV with Jenny yelling, "Push publish!"

My hands were shaking. I had a split second to make a decision to tranq Fiona or push publish. I saved the recording and found the publish button, praying I made the right decision.

A gunshot shattered the silence in the living quarters, instantly followed by Jenny's piercing scream and the heavy thud of a body hitting the floor. *I'd made the wrong decision.*

CHAPTER 21
THE FALSE ENDING

I FROZE, my heart thundering in my chest. The faint metallic tang of blood in my mouth from biting my lip mingled with the faint scent of coffee lingering from earlier. I could barely breathe, forcing each shallow gulp of air past the knot of fear rising in my throat. Fiona's voice echoed in my mind, calm but chilling, like she'd switched off any hint of humanity.

If I stepped out into the living room, she'd likely shoot me too, no hesitation. But my best friend lay there, possibly bleeding out, and I couldn't just leave her. The air was thick and pressing, and every second felt like a punch to my gut. My hands trembled, sticky with sweat. If I stayed back here, she'd find me anyway. She'd changed her mind about poison—she wanted to watch her victims fall one by one. My pulse thrummed louder. The choice hung heavy in the silence —stay hidden or face Fiona head-on. Either way, she was coming for me next.

"Haarperrr, get out here and help me!" Jenny yelled.

I stepped from behind the black curtain that separated the two spaces, prepared for the worst.

Jenny sat on the floor next to Fiona's body. "I didn't mean to shoot her. She was coming for you and we wrestled on the floor…"

"This is the police! Come out with your hands up and place your weapons on the ground." A glaring white light shone into the RV windows.

"Is she dead?" I asked.

"I don't know. I can't find any blood."

Fiona's eyes were closed. She looked dead. I reached for her wrist and took her pulse. "She's still alive."

"I repeat. Come out with your hands up." The flashing lights took another pass over the RV.

"Is that a helicopter?" Jenny asked. "I didn't know Evergreen Heights had one."

"We need to go out and surrender ourselves so Fiona can get medical attention." I pulled Jenny away from Fiona's body.

"Come on, she's not dead, and it's not like she is going to go anywhere."

Jenny and I stumbled out of the RV into the snow with our hands over our heads. She placed Fiona's gun on a snowbank. I put the tranq gun beside us as the lights took another pass.

"Where are they going to land?" Jenny asked.

"They're not going to land," I said. "That's a drone."

"Jake, if you can hear me, we need the police and an ambulance," I yelled at the drone.

The drone hovered over us and then Jenny's phone buzzed with a text from Jake:

The police are on their way.

I sighed. It was over. I'd released the podcast and likely the whole town was listening to it. The drone circled one last time before heading out of the campground. Jake must be sure that help is on the way. Faint sirens hummed in the distance, getting closer. I picked up the tranq gun.

"I'm going to put this back and check on Fiona."

I opened the RV door and Fiona knocked me to the ground. I fell on my butt as she took off toward Hemlock Trail. The sirens were in the parking lot now, but the police wouldn't be here soon enough to catch Fiona. She knew these woods like the back of her hand. If she escaped, she could hide out for days.

With one hand, I pushed myself off the ground and, on my knees, I aimed the tranq gun and fired, hitting her square in the back. She went over in slow motion, plopping on the ground spread-eagle like a toddler wearing too much bulky snow gear.

Detective Dexter burst through the trees with a flashlight. He scanned the scene before landing on Fiona's still form.

"Did you…" he said, not finishing what he was thinking.

"No. I shot her," Jenny said, while dusting the snow off her pants. "But for some reason it didn't take."

"I just tranqed her," I added.

"Yeah, thanks Poindexter for rushing over here to rescue us," Jenny said, before turning to me. "Let's get you home, Harper."

Dexter stepped between Jenny and me and rubbed his hands over my coat sleeves. "Are you hurt?"

"No. I'm fine," I replied and smiled a crinkly I'm-about-to-melt-down smile.

"I'm fine too, thanks for asking," Jenny stated, as she grabbed my shoulder and pulled me out of the hug. "Let's get out of here."

A few more officers swarmed the scene while paramedics loaded Fiona on an ambulance stretcher.

"Detective, look at this," a paramedic offered. He waved a National Audubon Society thick field guide in the air. "This was in her flannel pocket and it has a bullet in it."

"Wait," Dexter said. "You two can't leave. I need to get your statements."

"Just listen to the podcast," Jenny said. "If you need to ask us anything else, we will be at Harper's celebrating solving the case."

Jenny had suddenly gotten motherly and protective. Maybe my aunt was rubbing off on her. Or maybe God was saving me from melting down in front of the town's entire police and EMS departments.

Jenny turned on her phone flashlight and linked arms with me.

"Oh, and the laptop and Elmer's research are all on the table in the RV," I added over my shoulder to Dexter. Then we trudged through the snow, breathing in deep calming breaths and admiring the stars.

———

As we pushed open the door to my apartment, an explosion of homemade confetti greeted us, floating down in a flurry of neon paper scraps and glitter that sparkled in the dim hallway light. The Murder Club erupted in cheers, their voices bouncing off the walls and filling the room with a warmth I hadn't realized I was craving. I felt the relief settle over me, loosening the tightness in my chest.

"You solved the case and caught the murderer!" Robin's voice broke through the noise as she practically bounced toward me, her face flushed with excitement.

I shrugged off my coat, my muscles still stiff from the lingering adrenaline, and hung it on the hook. "Not before she almost caught us," I said, brushing bits of confetti from my hair.

Jenny crossed her arms with a wry grin. "I *did* have to shoot her, after all."

"Wait—she's *dead*?" Cassy's eyes went wide, and she shivered, wrapping herself tighter in her oversized cardigan.

"Nope," Jenny said, shaking her head. "She had a National Audubon Society thick field guide in her flannel breast pocket. Guess she was prepared for bird watching *and* murder."

I felt Zoe's hand squeeze my shoulder, grounding me like she could sense I needed her steady presence after everything.

"Well, I *did* tranq her," I added, smirking a little. The tranquilizer dart had been my idea, one that thankfully worked.

I knew Jenny would take over telling the rest of the story with a follow-up podcast, and she'd probably play up her heroics. That was fine. We were both alive, Fiona was in custody, and I was surrounded by friends.

"This is the *coolest* club ever," Ethan said, running

his fingers through his confetti-covered hair with a grin that made his eyes sparkle.

From the kitchen, Aunt Mary appeared, holding a cake crowned with sparklers. The smell of vanilla and warm sugar filled the room. She beamed, her eyes glistening with pride as she set the cake down and pulled out a bouquet of balloons from behind her. "You *did* it!"

I could feel the laughter bubbling up as I looked around at each of them, my oddball family. The confetti, the cheers, the sweetness of cake—it all hit me at once. We'd faced down danger and come out on the other side.

There was a knock at the door, which was hard to hear because of all the noise. I excused myself from Zoe's grip and answered it.

"Dexter," I said.

"I need to ask you and Jenny a few questions."

"I'm kind of in the middle of a party."

Jenny joined me at the door. I hadn't let him in yet. I didn't want to. I'd rather he go and keep his opinions about me to himself.

Jenny put both hands on her hips like a superhero. "We solved the case for you *again.*"

"Oh, Harper," Cara said as she squeezed by Dexter. "Thanks for clearing my name."

Aunt Mary joined us at the door. "Cara, Dexter, come in and have some cake."

"I'm here on official business," Dexter said.

"Oh pooh. It's a small town. These girls solved Elmer's murder. Come in and celebrate. You can ask them questions later."

"Or you can listen to the podcast," Jenny said. "She confesses everything."

Dexter shrugged his shoulders in defeat. He wasn't winning this argument with my aunt.

"There is still one loose end," I said as I linked arms with Jenny and Zoe shoved a mug of coffee in my hand.

"Come sit, Boss," Zoe said, pointing to the sectional.

I sat down and set my coffee down. "Cara's money, and I think I know where it might be."

"You do?" Dexter sat down next to me. Aunt Mary had already dished up a piece of cake. He held his fork, poised to dig in.

"Not exactly *where*. But it was something Fiona said."

"What was that?"

"Fiona said, 'We're going to walk out into the woods and no one will find your bodies until spring.'"

The college students moved closer, leaning in.

"She said that? She was going to kill you both," Cassy said, clutching her coffee with both hands.

Jake replied, "The probability that they were going to get out of there alive was—"

Robin punched Jake. "But you used your drone and saved the day."

"Actually, I shot Fiona and saved the day," Jenny said.

I interrupted. "Thank you, Jake. Did you see us run out with our hands up and drop our weapons in the snow?"

Ethan answered, "We did, on your big screen TV. It was so cool. Like a movie."

"Yeah," Ryan added. "Like an action movie." He

hummed the theme song for *Mission Impossible* and danced around like he had a gun in his hand. It was the most animated and alive I'd seen him since he signed up for my class.

Dexter turned to Jake, his voice sharp and direct. "Do you have the footage?"

Jake nodded, already pulling out his phone. "Of course, I'll send you the file." He tapped the screen a few times, then glanced up. "Done."

I sighed, running a hand through my hair as I thought back to the moment. "I shouldn't have tranqed her," I muttered, shaking my head. "I should have let her go."

Aunt Mary reached over, patting my hand reassuringly before sliding the cake platter toward me. "You did what you had to do, Harper," she said, in her usual matter-of-fact tone. "Now, have another piece of cake. It'll help."

Ethan's eyes lit up, his mouth dropping open in awe as he looked at me. "That's so cool. You tranqed her," he said, practically bouncing in his seat.

"No. Not cool," Dexter and I said at the same time, for very different reasons I'm sure.

I couldn't help but laugh, even though I still felt a hint of guilt. "Let's just say it was a last resort, Ethan," I replied, trying to keep it light.

"I thought we were talking about Cara's money," Zoe said, getting the conversation back on track.

"We are. Indirectly. I can explain." I stood and walked to the murder board. I pointed at Fiona and then moved her picture to the top of the board.

"Fiona is much smarter than anyone gives her credit for." I tapped her photo for emphasis. "Don't be fooled by those natural good looks, braids, and freckles, which make her look younger and more naïve than she really is."

"So she masterminded everything?" Robin asked, leaning forward.

"Not exactly…" I paused, choosing my words carefully. Most of The Murder Club only knew Fiona from the lecture she led in the woods. The beginning seemed the best place to start.

"I first met her when Dexter introduced her." I turned toward him, remembering that moment. "You told me Fiona is a do-it-yourself kind of person. Whether it's foraging for food, repairing her gear, or navigating through the wilderness, she's highly self-reliant. If something breaks, she fixes it. If she needs something, she often makes it herself."

"Yes, but what does that have to do with anything else?" Robin pressed, frowning as she tried to connect the dots.

"I'm establishing her character," I replied with a nod. "What would a do-it-yourself kind of woman do when the forest she loves is threatened? Or her reputation in academia?"

Ryan leaned back with a skeptical look. "I still don't get it."

"She killed Elmer, silly," Zoe said, crossing her arms as if it were obvious. "To turn in his research as her own."

"There's more, isn't there?" Jenny leaned in, her eyes alight with interest. "Permission to record?" She held up her phone. "And can you repeat what Dexter told you about Fiona?"

"Yes, and yes." I repeated Dexter's description of Fiona and continued. "She figured out who Luther Weston was before us. She put together the whole con."

"And...?" Cara asked, her voice tense. "She was friends with my husband?"

"No. The opposite," I said, shaking my head. "She told Jenny and me that Elmer was the one who found Luther in the woods and made sure he got proper medical treatment."

"Oh, Elmer..." Aunt Mary dabbed at her eyes with a tissue that Zoe passed to her.

Robin shook her head, her expression still puzzled. "I still don't get it."

"How would Fiona know that Elmer found Luther wounded in the woods?" I leaned forward, lowering my voice. "I think you'll find that Luther suffered a blunt force trauma to the back of the head."

"A blow that was meant to kill him," Jenny said, her face lighting up as she jumped up in excitement.

"Yes, but it didn't," I explained, watching the realization ripple through the room. "Elmer came along... and Fiona had to hide."

Cara's face hardened. "She took my money," she muttered. "But why?"

"Well," Zoe interjected with a shrug, "she couldn't exactly give it back to you and say, I tried to kill your husband and failed, but here's your money back."

"Right," I replied with a wry smile in Zoe's direction.

"But why did you say you shouldn't have tranqed

her?" Cassy asked, her gaze darting between Dexter and me.

"Because she would have gone to retrieve the money that no one will find until spring," Dexter replied, slipping into his detective tone with a small, knowing smile.

"So we need to find the place that thaws last. Like the highest point. Or where the snow drifts?" Jake said as he pulled out his laptop. "On it."

His fingers clacked on the keys as everyone sipped coffees and waited, except me. Ethan joined me at the board and rearranged the yarn, connecting everyone to Fiona.

"Got it," Jake said. "There's a cavern at the top of Redbird Falls. It's famous for having snow blocking the entrance until May."

"Oh, yeah," Zoe said she pulled out her phone. "Tourists post photos of snowball fights in May." she waved her phone around displaying blurry photos of people in short sleeves throwing snowballs at each other.

"Looks like I've got to organize another arrest and a search party." Dexter said. He set his dessert plate down and stood, wiping the crumbs off his pants, which Rory was happy to clean up.

"May I come and record?" Jenny asked.

"Come on, let Jenny go," Zoe said, snapping a few photos of Dexter and The Murder Club. "Local murder club solves murder and attempted murder, plus a plot for con artists to take Christmas Tree Forest for all it's got." She paused and pulled Jenny next to Dexter and snapped twenty more photos. "Local curmudgeon detective refuses to let Jenny Murder, host of Crime-caster Podcast, ride along to witness the arrest. Yep. That'll do it."

"You can't post those," Dexter said, reaching for the camera.

"Freedom of the Press, baby," Zoe said, backing up.

"Yeah, Detective, legally we're good to go," Jake said, tapping away at his laptop. "First Amendment protects us here—freedom of the press, you know? Once someone's arrested, it's fair game to report on it."

The detective raised an eyebrow. "But couldn't it mess with the trial?"

"Well, that's where the Sixth Amendment kicks in," Jake replied, not missing a beat. "The court can order a gag if it thinks media coverage could mess with a fair trial, but usually that's on lawyers and cops. Podcasters like Jenny? She's free to talk—just gotta be careful she's not spreading lies, or, boom—defamation lawsuit."

"Noted," the detective said, leaning in. "So, Jenny's podcast is clear to run the story?"

"Absolutely," Jake nodded. "Just as long as she sticks to the facts.

Dexter's phone buzzed, and as he read the message, his jaw clenched. "Fiona escaped."

Jenny replied, "Well, looks like we know exactly where she's headed."

Everyone fell silent, tension rippling through the room.

"Where?" Ethan asked, his eyes sharp with antic-ipation.

"The cavern," Dexter replied, his voice grim. "She

stashed Luther's money there, and now she's going back for it."

Jenny's eyes lit up as she grabbed her phone. "A cavern chase with a murderer? This might be my best scoop yet."

Dexter shot her a look, but didn't slow down as he headed for the door. "If we hurry, we can cut her off before she makes a clean getaway."

He paused in the doorway, glancing back at The Murder Club. "This isn't over. Not by a long shot."

And with that, he walked out the door with Jenny, who rushed to grab her things and keep up.

CHAPTER 22

UNDER THE STARS, A NEW BEGINNING

THE MURDER CLUB hung out at my apartment, waiting on news from Jenny or Dexter that they found Fiona and the case was over. Aunt Mary took Cara back to her house to wait there. Zoe and Cassy cleaned up the kitchen. I sat in my reading chair and leaned my head back with Rory at my feet. The boys sat on the sectional talking about the case.

It felt like the case that never ends. What did Dexter mean, *this isn't over yet, not by a long shot?* Our relationship? His talking to The Murder Club about the meddling in his cases?

"I can't believe we missed—" My phone buzzed, cutting me off. I glanced down, my heart skipping as I saw the message from Jenny:

> We got Fiona. She led us right to the
> money.

A rush of relief and excitement surged through me. I

stood up, clearing my throat to get everyone's attention as I read the text aloud. "They got her, and they found the money."

The room erupted. Zoe punched the air, grinning like she'd won the lottery. "We solved the case, Boss!"

Ethan let out a low whistle, his eyes wide with disbelief. "We actually did it! A real case!" He drummed his hands on his thighs, unable to keep still. "Who else can say they helped catch a con artist and a murderer in the middle of a crime spree?"

Jake, ever the cool-headed tech whiz, tried to hold back a grin but failed miserably. "I mean, this whole thing could go viral. Just imagine the headlines…" He was already tapping furiously at his laptop, probably drafting an update for the social media account Zoe had created.

Cassy covered her mouth, her eyes gleaming with excitement. "I can't believe it," she whispered, her cheeks flushed. "Our little club actually cracked a real case. Harper, this is… unreal." She clutched my arm, her hand warm and trembling.

Robin looked stunned as she paced the room, running a hand through her hair. "This is nuts!" she said, her voice almost a laugh. "I mean, I know we hoped we'd solve it, but…" She looked around, a slow smile spreading across her face. "We actually did. *We* did."

And then there was Ryan, who had been quiet, just watching the group with a thoughtful expression. Finally, he broke into a wide smile, shaking his head. "Honestly, Harper, I didn't think we'd pull this off," he admitted, chuckling. "It feels like we're in one of those true crime shows. Except this time, we're the ones who cracked it."

I took a steadying breath, letting the moment sink in. The faint smell of coffee hung in the air, mingling with the sweet scent of vanilla from the cake Aunt Mary had brought over. The excited hum of the group vibrated around me. My pulse began to settle, a comforting warmth filling my chest.

As I looked around at each of them—my unlikely team, my friends—I realized we'd pulled off something incredible.

After the group had settled, Zoe closed the dishwasher she'd been loading. "Alright, everyone, time to head out—like a snowplow through a blizzard! My boss needs to rest."

Five minutes later, everyone moved in slow motion like snowplows slipping on the ice. Each of them rehearsed their part in the case. Finally, The Murder Club cleared the building.

I sat on the couch while Zoe ordered us some dinner.

"Hey why are you staying?" I asked, while wrapping my favorite blanket around me.

"Because Edgar loves you and all, but you can't keep calling him in the middle of the night when you have an episode."

"He thinks I'm going to have an episode?" I asked. I rearranged the mustard colored blanket across my legs.

"No offense, Boss, but you had one at the funeral. You just got out of bed today and you were just held at gunpoint." She reached for my hand and held it.

"Why are you holding my hand? I'm not a child."

"Edgar said, and I quote, 'Zoe, watch for the signs. If Harper's voice starts to shake, or she keeps rubbing her hands, she's on edge. And if she starts looking around too fast or her breathing gets shallow, she's close to a panic attack.'"

"Zoe, you are not going to sit here and hold my hand all night." I pulled my hand away.

"Harper, would you rather Dexter hold your hand?" She laughed.

"No. Yes. I don't want to talk about that."

"Did you have another argument?"

"No. We had the same argument," I said.

"Which one?"

"The one where he says real investigators share every clue. Not mystery writers posing as them."

"Why would he say that? You have solved every case he's had since he moved to town."

"Well, right after we kiss—"

Zoe jumped up and danced around the living room. "You kissed?" Rory joined her.

"I'm not telling you anything else until you order us some food. I'm starving."

Zoe stopped mid-dance. "That's food blackmail."

"Whatever it is, I'm not saying another word about the K-word until I know I have a bacon avocado burger and sweet potato fries on the way."

Zoe placed the order and paced while the food was on the way. I curled up on the couch and pretended to be asleep while I rehearsed in my head what I would say to her concerning the K-word.

Once our food arrived, I told her the whole story.

"I knew Jenny was going to talk about the note she

received on the next podcast, but knowing her, she hadn't shared it with the police," I began.

Then I told her about the kiss, which I made sure sounded like an innocent peck on the mouth, and then the unfeeling text directly following.

"That's it?"

"No. There's more. When I got the weird text after the snowstorm, and the electricity buzzed, we were about to put an extraterrestrial on the board as a suspect."

"I knew that would freak you out, so I texted you and explained it." She laughed and then stuffed a sweet potato fry in her mouth.

"After everyone left, I called Dexter to fill him in on the note Jenny received," I told Zoe, trying to keep my tone casual. "I even sent him a screenshot and the text itself."

Zoe's eyebrows shot up. "Oh, I bet he loved that."

I nodded, a wry smile tugging at the corner of my mouth. "He wasn't thrilled, let's say that. First, he huffed. Then there was this solid three seconds of silence. Finally, he asked, 'Why didn't you tell me about the typed note earlier?'"

"Oh, please," Zoe said, folding her arms with a shake of her head. "Like you could've squeezed that in."

"I tried explaining that I *had* gone back to the car to tell him, but..." I hesitated, feeling my cheeks warm at the memory.

"But he kissed you first," she finished, smirking like she'd guessed my secret.

"Yes, and honestly, who follows up a kiss like that

with, 'Oh, by the way, Jenny Murder got a typed note related to the case'? I mean, it's not exactly pillow talk," I said, still feeling the sting of how the conversation had gone.

"And what did Mr. Wonderful say to that?" Zoe asked, leaning in, her eyes gleaming with amusement.

I sighed. "He said, 'Real investigators, that's who. Not mystery writers posing as them.' Just like that—full of frustration. And it hurt, Zoe. I thought maybe we'd turned a corner, you know?"

She rolled her eyes, exhaling sharply. "So he's back to doubting you? Typical."

"Then he says I should stop investigating, disband The Murder Club, the whole works."

Zoe's expression turned serious. "And I'm sure you told him where he could take that suggestion," she said, a proud gleam in her eyes.

"Let's just say I kept my composure," I replied. "I asked if that was an order from the police department or from him personally."

Zoe grinned, seeing where this was going. "And?"

"When he said it was from *him*, I told him I was ignoring it. And then I hung up," I said, folding my arms, feeling that spark of pride flare up again.

She laughed, nodding with approval. "Nice, Harper. He may be the detective, but you're the one who actually gets things done."

We finished dinner and Zoe cleaned up again while I camped out on the sectional, watching *You've Got Mail*.

"I'm going to walk Rory," she said when she finished wiping the table.

As soon as she left, the air in the room shifted. My

hands started trembling, a slow, insistent shake I couldn't control. I stared at them, but they didn't feel like mine—my fingers tingled, numb and strange, as if they'd forgotten how to listen to me.

I gasped, but my lungs refused to work. The room closed in, walls pressing closer and closer, the silence around me amplifying each missed breath. I rolled off the sectional, gripping the floor to ground myself, curling up as tight as I could. If I stayed still, maybe the world would stop spinning. Maybe I'd find a way to breathe again.

———

Edgar had been right. I spent another two days in bed under my weighted blanket.

Dexter stopped by one afternoon, his presence heavier than usual. He sat down on the bed with a thud instead of taking the chair. His eyes crinkled at the edges, the sincerity in them unmistakable. His dark mop of hair was messier than usual, as if he'd been running his hands through it all day in frustration. I caught a faint trace of his cologne—something woodsy and warm—hinting at the scents of winter.

"I'm sorry I said you weren't a real investigator. You are," he said, his voice quieter than normal, almost hesitant.

I fluffed my pillows, propping myself up straighter, and folded my hands in front of me to keep them from trembling. Not out of fear, but nerves—relationship nerves. Is that a thing? Could someone be nervous about something so... possible?

"Thank you for apologizing," I said finally, my voice steadier than I felt. "That really hurt. But I've realized it hurt more because of things my mom and dad have said to me in the past." My hands clenched together briefly before I forced myself to relax them.

Dexter frowned, his gaze searching mine, and then he raked a hand through his hair again, leaving it even wilder. "I didn't mean to hit a nerve," he admitted. "I was just worried about you. I don't want you to get hurt because... then what would I do? Blame myself? Or worse, what if Fiona had killed you?" His voice cracked slightly. "I'd be devastated."

I stared at him, my breath catching. "You would?"

"Yes, Harper. I care about you a lot. Enough to rent the apartment across the street...if you approve."

"You need my approval?"

His lips quirked up in a small, sheepish smile. "I'd like it. It doesn't make sense for me to rent it if you're not in my life." He reached out, gently brushing a stray curl out of my face before his fingers lingered along my cheek, warm and rough.

A jolt of electricity sparked where his fingers touched, racing down my neck to my chest, leaving my heart hammering as if it might burst.

Instead of doing something appropriate—like kissing him, hugging him, or even grabbing his hand— my mind latched onto the fact that I hadn't brushed my teeth. Or my hair.

"I can't see it today," I said, patting my weighted blanket for emphasis, as if it explained everything.

But then Cassy's advice echoed in my mind: *relationships mean meeting each other's needs*. And this? This mattered. He knew I hadn't showered, brushed my teeth, or even swiped deodorant in all the right places, yet here he was—apologizing.

I reached out, taking his hand in mine and pulling him gently toward me. His warmth felt grounding, steadying. We didn't kiss. We didn't need to. The hug was enough. It sealed the apology, the moment, and whatever we were becoming. For now, it was enough to put us firmly in the more-than-casual category.

A week later, I'd resumed my regular schedule, including helping with story hour, visiting with The Classics, book club, and teaching. It felt good to be back.

Edgar and I had a few extra sessions to talk through what had happened in my body and work on some new techniques. As long as there wasn't a new murder, I didn't think I would need them.

Jenny was off at The Truth & Crime Awards in Grandview City for her Crimecaster episode of an actual murderer's confession. I had listened to the podcast. True to form, she'd edited me almost completely out. The governor sent me an invite too, but I declined, much to my mother's horror. She threatened to hop on a plane and attend with me, but I sent Sage instead. She'd written an award-winning piece on the Westons and Fiona, as well as Elmer's work on the Cerulean Warbler and a slight nod to The Murder Club helping to solve the case.

———

The stars twinkled brightly in the navy blue sky, a sparkling blanket that seemed to stretch infinitely above us. I leaned back in my camping chair, the crisp air filling my lungs, and watched my breath plume out like a small cloud of vapor in the chill of the night. The crackling campfire cast flickering shadows on our faces, adding warmth to the cool evening.

"Can you believe it?" Cara's animated voice cut through the peaceful sounds of the forest. "I actually got my money back! The state is going to open a wildlife interactive museum for kids on my land!" She beamed at us, her excitement radiating like the fire's glow.

"That's amazing, Cara!" I said, smiling back at her. "Your new vision for the property is coming to life!"

"Just think of all the kids who will get to learn about nature up close," Zoe added, her eyes sparkling in the firelight. She wrapped her arms around her knees, leaning forward with genuine enthusiasm. "You've turned your experience into something so positive."

Aunt Mary, seated across from us, clapped her hands together. "I can't wait to see what you do with the place! It'll be like a little slice of magic out here," she said, her voice rich with warmth. "You've always had such a gift for bringing people together, Cara."

"Speaking of magic," Dexter said, nodding toward the woods where a shadow approached. "I think someone just joined our circle."

Anora stepped into the light, her presence instantly commanding yet approachable. Her long, glossy hair fell in loose waves down her back, and her sun-kissed skin glowed softly in the firelight. A practical yet chic ponytail kept her hair neatly in place, and her bright, expressive eyes sparkled with curiosity as she took in our gathering.

"Hope I'm not interrupting," Anora said, her smile reflecting her adventurous spirit. "I wanted to come by and celebrate this wonderful news with all of you. Cara, the museum is a fantastic idea!"

Cara's face lit up, and she gestured for Anora to join us. "Thanks, Anora! I'm so excited. It's a chance for kids to engage with nature in a fun way, and you're welcome to help however you'd like!"

"I'd love to," Anora replied, settling onto a log near the fire. "With my role at the DNR, I can help connect you with resources and programs that will enhance the museum experience."

Dexter shifted closer to me, intertwining our fingers as he looked at Anora. "We were just brainstorming ideas about how to incorporate storytelling workshops into the museum's programs. What do you think?"

"That sounds incredible," Anora said, nodding enthusiastically. "Stories have a powerful way of teaching lessons about the environment. I can see it now—kids learning about wildlife while creating their own narratives."

Zoe chimed in, her excitement infectious. "And we could use social media to share their stories, maybe even create a blog to highlight their experiences!"

Aunt Mary chuckled, her gaze shifting to the fire. "You all have such bright ideas. Just remember, there's nothing quite like a campfire story to spark a child's imagination."

"Speaking of stories," Dexter said, glancing at me

with a playful smile. "Did I tell you about the time I got lost hiking in the woods?"

"Oh no, not that one again!" Zoe laughed, rolling her eyes playfully. "I think you've told us that one a hundred times."

I squeezed Dexter's hand, loving the way he could turn a simple moment into an adventure. "But it's such a good story," I teased, looking at him with affection. "Let's hear it again!"

Cara leaned back in her chair, grinning as she settled in for a tale. "I'm all ears," she said, brushing back a strand of hair that had escaped her ponytail.

As Dexter launched into his story, describing the twists and turns of his journey through the woods, I felt a sense of contentment wash over me. The laughter, the camaraderie, and the shared dreams floated around us like the smoke curling up into the starry sky. We were creating our own little world here, and I couldn't help but feel hopeful for everything that lay ahead.

ABOUT THE AUTHOR

Kathleen Guire is the mother of seven, four through adoption, NiNi of fourteen, former National Parent of the Year, author, teacher, and speaker. She loves connecting with readers through her website (Kathleen guireauthor.com).

For more information,
about Kathleen, check out her website and follow her
on social media!
www.kathleenguireauthor.com
kathleenguire@gmail.com
https://linktr.ee/kguire

ALSO BY KATHLEEN GUIRE

If you missed it, grab the first two books in the series:

Fatal Fixer-Upper: A Christian Cozy Mystery of Murder, Suspense, and Reality TV (Cozy Corner Mysteries Book 1)

Crimecaster Cold Case: A Christian Cozy Mystery in the Pursuit of a Serial Killer (Cozy Corner Mysteries Book 2)